I0824436

Pioneering in the Pampas

RICHARD ARTHUR SEYMOUR

with a preface by

Juan Carlos Casas

STOCKCERO

910.4 SEY

Seymour, Richard
Pioneering in the Pampa's.- 1ª. ed.–
Buenos Aires : Stock Cero, 2002.
156 p. ; 23x16 cm.

ISBN 987-20506-6-X

I. Título - 1. Relatos de Viajes

FIRST PUBLISHED IN LONDON (1869)

by LONGMANS, GREEN, AND CO.

1º edición: 2002
Stockcero
ISBN Nº 987-20506-6-X
Libro de Edición Argentina.

Hecho el depósito que prevé la ley 11.723.
Printed in the United States of America.

stockcero.com
Viamonte 1592 C1055ABD
Buenos Aires Argentina
54 11 4372 9322

stockcero@stockcero.com

Pioneering in the Pampas

or

THE FIRST FOUR YEARS

OF

A SETTLER'S EXPERIENCE IN THE LA PLATA CAMPS

by

RICHARD ARTHUR SEYMOUR

with a preface by

JUAN CARLOS CASAS

STOCKCERO

PREFACE TO THE PRESENT EDITION

Should the reader of this book expect a literary masterpiece, he is bound for disappointment.

Richard Seymour was not a master writer. However, his love for detail and outstanding memory captivates with the educated and fluent prose of an "average" nineteenth century Oxford scholar.

Vivid descriptions about the terrible Ranqueles Indians faces, the Gauchos outfits, and the differences between Indian and Gaucho horse taming methods make reading Pioneering in the Pampas a journey into the experience of everyday life at the Pampas Indian frontier during the mid eighteen hundreds.

Minutiae such as hand brick-making, how many bricks per day an experienced worker could make, and how much would he do before becoming exhausted –all basic matters assuming that, even in the midst of nowhere, prime among your goals stands living like an English esquire– dot the book.

Were the gauchos honest workers or did they try to work as little as possible? How were the English-type horse races held in Rosario organized? All questions that haunted the earnest Victorian gentleman are subject to Mr. Richard Seymour's sharp observations.

Among the both practical and curious details stand:

- The outrageously high labour wages –compared to those at home– cowhands, brick makers, horse breakers, and others.
- The weak commitment to religion of the Gauchos, who "delegated" church attendance to women leaving to them the chores of advocating on their behalf at doomsday.
- The exaggerated size up to which vegetables grew, to much-surprise of the Englishmen.
- How commonplace it was for newcomers travelling in the Pampas to lose track of time, ending up sleeping in the open, as Hume and a friend experienced the harsh way.

- The high-rank inhabitants of a low-rank town, such as Fraile Muerto in those days, including the town's cheap hotel and its colourful clientele.
- Differences between Creole and English sheep.
- The immediate requirement to dig trenches surrounding the houses and corrals as a defence measure against Indian attacks.
- The ill-fated government decision to transfer the soldiers from the line of forts, thus leaving unprotected the white population south of the Córdoba Province.
- The appearance of cholera in the region and its high death toll.
- How law and order were enforced by the "comandante" through summary trials and executions, and why English pioneers always carried their revolvers.

Through Richard Seymour's narrative, the geography of the Pampas and the times before railroads and immigration waves acquire amazingly realistic characteristics.

Soon enough the conquest of the desert by President Roca in 1880 would change the character of the place, though strangely Richard Seymour seems unwilling to stand witness to it. Without explicitly mentioning the detail in his book, he departed for England in1869 where –in the Rectory of Kinwarton, Warwickshire– he devotedly relived his experiences by writing this book.

The vivid memories and the ever present strict Victorianism of his stance regarding relations with the opposite sex, strikingly never mentioned in spite of his youth and circumstance –a man in his early twenties dwelling with bachelor friends in a savage land where they must have undoubtedly encountered Creoles, Indians and some scarce British female subjects– altogether with the implicitly painful and unexplained abandonment of it all, sparked my mind up to the point of writing "Fraile Muerto", the novel, bridging the notorious sex absence gap with an imaginary underlying plot.

All said, I must add that bringing back to print Richard Seymour's book is my most sincere homage to the man who preceded me in the love for the strange solitudes of the Argentine Pampa's soul.

Juan Carlos Casas
Buenos Aires – December 2002

TO THE

HON. GERALD C. TALBOT

and

REV. R. SEYMOUR,

In grateful recollection

of

THEIR WARM AND CONSTANT INTEREST IN

THE SETTLERS AT MONTE MOLINO

PREFACE.

The writer of the following pages is well aware that the only apology that is worth anything for the publication of a book must be found in its contents. If his readers do not find these such as to justify the presumption which asks for their perusal, no preface, however ingenious, can be of any worth. And yet he is anxious to bespeak the favour of those under whose eyes this volume may chance to fall, by briefly saying, that while he grants the superior merits, in almost every respect, of such works on the La Plate regions as Mr. Hinchcliff´s, Mr. Hutchinson's, Mr. Latham's, and though last in its appearance, by no means least in value, the work of Señor Sarmiento, the present enlightened President of the Argentine Republic, the claim of this volume, if it has any claim at all, lies in this - that the ground it traverses has been scarcely touched by those writers, inasmuch as it is confined almost exclusively to the simple narration of the difficulties which beset the settler in the first few years of his enterprise, more particularly when he has been tempted to fix himself outside the older settlements, and to be, as in the case of the writer and his companions, in the truest sense of the word, a Pioneer.

R. A. S.

KINWARTON RECTORY:
August 25, 1869.

CHAPTER I.

VOYAGE OUT - LISBON - BAHIA - RIO - ARRIVE AT BUENOS AYRES.

I sailed from Liverpool, January 17, 1865, in the Kepler, bound for Buenos Ayres, intending to join a friend who had already been for a year and a half in the Argentine Republic, where we both hoped to make a rapid fortune by sheep-farming; how far these sanguine prospects have been realised I am now about to relate. I think also that a slight sketch of the difficulties, disappointments, and successes of a settler's life, in the River Plate, may not be wholly devoid of interest.

I went on board early in the morning and about ten o'clock we started. It was a cold raw day, and as we slowly steamed down the Mersey, I was glad, as soon as I lost sight of the friends who had come to see me off, to go below, and examine into my prospects of probable comfort during the voyage. These appeared rather promising, as, our number of passengers not being very large, I was favoured with a cabin to myself, opening on the saloon.

I was not able to indulge in much sentiment about the last sight of old England, as she was wrapped in her usual veil of fog; and if Lord Byron's celebrated "Farewell" had occurred to my mind, I must have bid "Adieu" not to blue but to brown water. The weather, however, on the whole, was very favourable, and we steamed rapidly along. I was much relieved by discovering myself to be a far better sailor than I expected, and, until subjected to the severe test of the Bay of Biscay, imagined myself quite impervious to the "Maladie de mer". But once well embarked on those stormy waters, we experienced some really rough weather, and very few of the passengers appeared at dinner on the first day. My chief amusement just then consisted in watching the large shoals of porpoises that used to play round the vessel, quite regardless of the rough state of the weather. I tried some shots at them with a revolver, but am happy to reflect that I did not succeed in abridging their ungainly existence, as porpoises are not among the delicacies usually served up on board ship, and necessity had not then reconciled me to the many varieties of food of which I have since partaken.

On the 24th we sighted the lighthouse just outside the Tagus, but for a day and a half the fog continued so thick that it was not till the afternoon of the second day that we could venture to cross the bar, and even then were forced to run in without a pilot. This delay did not sweeten the tempers of either officers or passengers, and many phrases which might be called strictly nautical were employed on this trying occasion. Once fairly over the bar, however, all annoyances were forgotten, or only enhanced our admiration of the beautiful view before us. The weather was lovely, and the banks on each side of the river, covered with verdure, made one conscious of having reached a more sunny clime. The most striking feature, however, on the banks of the Tagus, to the less poetical stranger who now beheld them for the first time, was the enormous quantity of small windmills; the cause of this I have been unable to discover for certain, but the unflattering reason I have heard assigned is that the Portuguese millers are such thieves that everyone is obliged to turn miller on his own account and grind his own corn for himself. I may just hint, by the way, that in my own beloved country I have heard a proverb which appears to throw a doubt on the integrity of other millers besides those on the banks of the Tagus -

Give me a miller that will not steal,
Give me a webster that is leal,
Find me a clerk that is not greedy,
And lay these three a dead corpse by;
And by virtue of these three
The same dead corpse shall quickened be.

We soon passed Cintra, which stands back at some little distance from the river and is beautifully situated among the hills, but the mist, though partially dissipated, prevented our seeing it at all clearly. About two miles below Lisbon stands Belem Castle, an old fortress, part of which appears to be of very ancient date; here the coast-guard boat and also that of the captain of the port boarded us, to carry out the vexatious quarantine regulations, which we were luckily able to escape on showing our clean bill of health. We then proceeded up the Tagus, and soon anchored close to Lisbon.

Here we were shortly joined by the Herschel, one of the same line of steamers as the Kepler, but homeward bound, and found, to our surprise, that she had on board the crew of II.M.S. Bombay, the flag-ship at Monte Video, which had just been unfortunately burnt, and was bringing them back to England. I found amongst them several officers to whom I had letters, which I had not expected to deliver so speedily.

We landed almost immediately and went up to the Braganza hotel, and, having established ourselves there, we proceeded to lionise Lisbon. The town is built on a number of little hills, the natural result of which is that most of the streets are very steep. The recollection of the dreadful earthquake appears still to be very vivid in the minds of the inhabitants of Lisbon, as I was told that the houses are still constructed to suffer as little as possible from a similar misfortune, the walls being built with a sort of wooden frame into which the lime and stones are tightly pounded down.

The streets are very well paved, and there are some fine squares. One called by the English sailors "Rolling Motion Square" is paved in a most peculiar manner with black and white stones, arranged in such a way as to have the appearance (more especially by moonlight) of small waves. The Opera House is very fine, and the performance of "La Marta", which we attended, was good.

We left Lisbon on the afternoon of the 25th with a fair wind, and in a few days sighted Palma, one of the Canary Islands; but we unfortunately passed the Peak of Teneriffe at night, so that we saw nothing of it. Our weather was beautiful, and the night splendid, as it was just then full moon. The stars have a friendly look to the traveller at sea, being the only perfectly familiar objects on which his eye can rest, and the faithful "Orion" carries him back to calm English summer nights, or frosty winter evenings, when he has shone above him in other, and well-remembered scenes. But even here there is a change, and the "Southern Cross", did not equal my expectations, nor in my opinion can it at all be compared to the old "Great Bear". We generally had some singing in the evenings; one of the passengers played the violin, and another the flute. There being only one lady on board, dancing was not very practicable. I also amused myself with my Spanish studies, and embarked upon "Gil Blas". We went through the usual ceremonies on passing the Line, some of the new hands on board being favoured with a visit from old Father Neptune; the passengers escaped an introduction to this venerable god by paying the usual fine. In spite of these innocent relaxations, I found the voyage very tedious, and was not sorry to arrive at Bahia, which we did on the 14th of February.

We landed at once, and in spite of the intense heat most of its directly set off for a walk of some miles, after the manner of Englishmen; some of our company, however, fell into the ways of the country at once, and were conveyed in the sedan-chairs or the place, called cadheras. The public gardens are pretty, and there is a beautiful view from them over the blue waters of the bay. I gathered some pods of a very pretty flower, a creeper, with blossoms something like a pea in shape, but of a pale blue colour, and sent them home, where I believe they grow well in a conservatory. The first sight of tropical plants and flowers must strike everyone much, and the white buildings of the town looked intensely hot and dazzling in the glaring sun. I went into the cathedral, which was most splendidly decorated: there were silver candlesticks and candelabra, and the shrines covered with gold lace, &c. There were some very fine frescoes on the roof, and in a sort of open court, outside, were some curious pictures of Scripture subjects on China tiles. Still Bahia in general is not a lovely town, the streets being narrow and ill-paved and very offensive to the olfactory nerves. We only remained there one night, and after another expedition into the country on the following morning to a place called Bamfu, sailed in the evening for Rio, feeling no great envy for one of our fellow-passengers who remained at Bahia.

We reached Rio de Janeiro on the 19th, and entered the harbour at about five o'clock in the morning, and having risen earlier than was my wont, to admire the entrance to the most beautiful harbour in the world, I was a good deal disgusted to find everything wrapped in a fog, so thick that we could see no farther than the bows of the ship. We consoled ourselves with breakfast, and on returning to the deck found that the fog had cleared away, and the lovely bay lay stretched before its in all its beauty. The Italians say "Vedi Napoli e poi mori", but the inventor of that proverb had certainly not seen Rio, as no national partialities can, I think, compare any harbour in the world to that which we now beheld. The entrance to the bay is very narrow, with the Sugar-loaf mountain rising straight out of the water on one side, and the fort on the other. Through this picturesque passage you come at once into the immense bay, more than sixty miles round. The wide expanse of blue water shone brightly in the morning sun as we slowly steamed in, and the magnificent background of mountains rose in the distance.

The town of Rio lies to the left as you enter the harbour, and is very picturesquely situated, many of the houses being dotted about among the thick tropical foliage of palm trees, plantains, &c. Behind the town rises the Corcovado mountain, and other hills stretch round to the right until they reach the Organ mountains, which are just above Petropolis, the favourite summer resort of the fashionable inhabitants of Rio. We soon landed, and agreed to spend most of our time in an expedition to Tijuca, a lovely spot among the mountains. After going about eight miles by train we procured mules, on which we rode to the hotel, and after ordering dinner there, we proceeded some four miles farther, along a winding path up the mountains, until we reached a beautiful waterfall surrounded with pines and flowers.

The sun was just setting as we returned to the hotel, and the view over the harbour, with the town stretched at our feet, the white shipping in the bay glowing in the departing light which lit up thc distant mountains with every imaginable tint of purple and gold, altogether made up a picture which must have been seen to be realised; and certainly no words of mine can adequately describe the lovely scene I then beheld. All around us was the most luxuriant vegetation in the world; orange-trees, bananas, palms, and tree-ferns towered above us, and the ground was carpeted with flowers of every colour, some of them extremely sweet; humming-birds and butterflies added to the brilliancy of the scene; some of the latter are immensely large, and I saw several which appeared to be about the size of an English thrush. But the whole place was to us like enchanted ground; and with every allowance for the feelings of travellers weary of the monotony of life on board ship and ready to think any spot of green earth a paradise, and also for the first dazzling effect of tropical scenery on the eyes of those hitherto accustomed to the gloomier colouring of our northern home, I think it is impossible that in this world there can be any other place so perfectly beautiful as Rio, nor can any description, either in poetry or prose, ever do it justice. I forgot to mention that at one of the houses near the waterfall I beheld something which delighted me even more than the large butterflies, one of which, by the bye, I vainly endeavoured to capture; this was a small ant-eater about the size of a little terrier dog, with a large bushy tail and a collar round its neck, so tame that it followed us about like a dog, and I should have much liked to carry it off with me. We spent the night at the hotel, and during the early part of it a most tremendous thunderstorm came on; the, lightning had a magnificent effect among the mountains, which it lit up most splendidly; and the violent rain was rather surprising to us after the drizzling showers of England, which certainly give no idea of what hard rain can be in the tropics. On returning to Rio next day, we went into the market, and were much amused by all the new beasts and birds which met our eyes; the gaily-coloured parrots and some lovely little marmosets especially took our fancy, to say nothing of the handsome negro women, slightly inclining to embonpoint, who looked very like bronzed statues in picturesque dresses.

Before returning to the ship I visited the cemetery appropriated to foreigners, which is about two miles out of the town and beautifully situated, lying at the foot of one of the hills, and running down almost to the water's edge. The graves are well kept, and I soon found the one I was in search of, which, like most of the others, was in a very good state; nor could anyone, I think, desire for those whom they most love a more beautiful and peaceful spot as their last resting-place than the burying-ground at Gamboya.

But we could not linger long on these delightful shores, and were soon tossing again on the waves of the Atlantic. We spent one night, the 30th, at Monte Video, the capital of the flourishing little republic of Uruguay, but, after Rio, the scenery was not very striking. The carnival was just going on, and I carried away a lively remembrance of the pastimes then practised, as some fair damsel dropped from a balcony upon my head a paper bag filled with water, which immediately burst and drenched me thoroughly. We reached Buenos Ayres about eight o'clock on the 2nd of March, and anchored so far out that my first view of my adopted country was a very indistinct one. The towers and spires of the churches were the only objects that broke the flat monotony of the distant view; but the most interesting sight to us was that of the whale-boats approaching to carry us to the shore, for the harbour is so shallow that a large ship is unable to approach nearer than five or six miles to Buenos Ayres. An enterprising speculator has recently proposed to remedy this, by reclaiming a large part of the inner roads, on condition that the recovered land shall belong to him; but for some reason or other he has at present been unable to agree with the Argentine Government as to the terms of the undertaking, and it seems to be abandoned. I soon entered one of the boats which were to convey us to the shore, and after about three hours row, under a very hot sun, was landed upon the mole, as the tide was then high; so we were not reduced to the usual ignominious expedient of landing in a cart, which is one of the customs of Buenos Ayres which strikes a stranger with some surprise.

CHAPTER II

BUENOS AYRES - VOYAGE UP THE URUGUAY - NIGHT IN A COAL HULK - FRAY BENTOS - GUALEGUAYCHU - FIRST IMPRESSIONS OF ENTRE RIOS.

If my accounts of settling in the River Plate strike my readers as being less "couleur de rose" than previous descriptions of the country which they may have read in the various interesting books already written by tourists in the Argentine Republic, it must be remembered how different are the impressions derived by the passing traveller, who, after perhaps the bustle and noise of a London season, spends a few pleasant holiday weeks among entirely new scenes, and visits the houses of long established and prosperous Estancieros, from the opinion of the same country formed by the new settler, who generally is forced to go to the very edge of civilisation in search of his fortune. The traveller, free from care, and with no thought in his mind but the enjoyment of the new scenes amidst which he finds himself, has simply to take his fill of the amusements which the hospitable Estanciero delights to provide for him. The settler, on the contrary, in the sort of locality which I am about to describe, with every possible disadvantage to contend against - of want of protection from Indians, want of timber, want of fuel, want of servants, and last of all, the great want which originally led him to fix his residence in a foreign country, want of money - endeavours slowly and with many hindrances to arrive at the same state of comfort and prosperity which has given the traveller so favourable an idea of the position of English settlers in the Argentine Republic.

I spent about five days in Buenos Ayres before proceeding up the country to join my friend, and received a good deal of kindness from several people to whom I had letters. A great deal of good advice was given me as to the best means of seeking my fortune; but opinions were divided on this point, some advising one part of the country, some another, and as there appeared not to be much safety in this multitude of counsellors, I was compelled to follow my own devices, and have since come to the conclusion that Experience is the only safe guide in the New as in the Old World, though unfortunately she costs nearly as much in the former as in the latter. The town of Buenos Ayres is built on a regular plan, that is to say, the houses are built in blocks of a hundred and fifty yards square; all the streets are therefore quite straight, and from the flat nature of the ground you can see a long way through them, a circumstance which prevents much picturesque beauty. The Plaza de la Victoria, with a statue erected to Victory in the middle or the square, is the finest part or the town, and here are also the cathedral and hall of justice. The immense amount of people on horseback strikes one directly, and it is rather a novel sight to an Englishman to see the number of horses standing every afternoon, quite unwatched, hobbled outside the Bolsa while their owners are transacting their business inside. Grooms are not much of an institution here, but the horses seem to understand their duty well, and stand perfectly still until their riders come out.

There are a good many wealthy English merchants in Buenos Ayres, and some of their houses are very handsome. I was not much charmed with my hotel, the internal arrangements of which seemed to show that cleanliness was not held in much esteem; but at this time I was more particular than becomes an Estanciero, and experience has taught me to be very thankful for much slenderer comfort.

On the 8th of March I started for Gualeguaychu in Entre Rios, one of the thirteen provinces of the Argentine Republic, situated between the rivers Parana and Uruguay, whence, as my intelligent reader will at once discover, is the origin of its name, Entre Rios. The city of Buenos Ayres is about three hundred miles from the sea, and is situated on the river La Plata, which, however, is here so enormously wide as rather to resemble a gulf than the mouth of a river. The La Plata is formed by the junction of the Parana and Uruguay, about fifty miles above Buenos Ayres; and the province of Buenos Ayres lies entirely to the south and west of the La Plata. Entre Rios and Corrientes are the only two provinces to the east of the Parana, the others all lying to the west; the two provinces between the rivers are therefore very well protected from the Indians, and being fertile, and possessing very good pasture for sheep and cattle, have become a favourite resort for settlers, and, with the exception of Buenos Ayres, are certainly the most thickly populated part of the whole republic. Land has consequently become very dear, and in the last four or five years has almost doubled its value. There are a great many flourishing Estancieros in Entre Rios, who have either made or are in a fair way to make large fortunes; but of course most of these have been here for a great many years, and began in the happy days when a small capital went farther in Entre Rios than it will do now.

I embarked in the steamer Era, and found a good many passengers on board; one of my companions in the Kepler was also going to Gualeguaychu, and there were several other young men bound on the same errand as myself; one of them, who had already been settled in the country some time, had come down to meet some friends, and cheered us with promising accounts of our new El Dorado. There were also some ladies on board whom I had met at Buenos Ayres, and being very nice people our voyage promised to be an agreeable one, and we all started in high spirits. We found we were to be accompanied by some of the conquerors of Paysandu, in the shape of several ferocious-looking soldiers in scarlet ponchos, whose general appearance was more picturesque than prepossessing. They were proceeding to the seat of war in the Banda Oriental, where the war between the Blancos and Colorados was then raging, and from the way in which they swaggered about, appeared anxious to impress us with their military character, nor did wee feel inclined to take any liberties with them.

We reached Fray Bentos at about twelve at night, and discovered that our destination there was a coal hulk, on board of which we were to wait for the small steamer for Gualeguaychu. Some accident appeared to have happened to this steamer, and we were informed she would not arrive till next day at the earliest. Report said that the accident consisted in the captain and chief engineer having made themselves ill by cating bad lobsters; at any rate, it was not until the following day that they were sufficiently recovered to resume their nautical duties. As we had nothing to eat or drink in our temporary sooty home, we composed ourselves to sleep on the boards, and very hard we found them. Our slumbers were not protracted very late into the following morning, and we went ashore rather early in search of breakfast. The town of Fray Bentos was not then at all striking; in fact, the plan hung up in the little hotel where we breakfasted, of the important city which sanguine owners of desirable lots of building land expected to see arise, reminded me strongly of the city of "Eden" in Martin Chuzzlewit; but since then I believe Fray Bentos has really grown very rapidly, and become an important place, as I see it described as such on the small pots of Liebig's extract of meat, which I find introduced into every well-regulated English household. But at the time of our visit the skeleton streets had a melancholy and curious effect, very different to any little rising English town; and not caring to linger in such an unattractive place, and finding there seemed to be no chance of the steamer's arrival, we engaged an English boatman to take us all up, with our lighter luggage, in a whaleboat, so called, I do not exactly know why, but certainly from no connection with the whale fishery.

We took about six hours to reach Gualeguaychu, and stopped sometimes to land and amuse ourselves by shooting ducks and partridges. The scenery along the banks of the river was rather pretty. Willows, orange trees, algaroba, and other trees, whose names I did not know, grew in great quantities, and the beautiful air plants, as they are called here, hung in profusion from the trees. It was very curious to see this hanging garden of lovely coloured plants, which would have been a perfect paradise to the possessors of English conservatories. The creepers, too, added to the effect, especially when, becoming creepers ourselves, we forced our way on hands and knees through the bushes, and found their long fibrous stems twining themselves round our arms and legs. We had provisioned the boat well, after our experience on board the hulk, and the expedition was more like a party of pleasure than a serious journey. We passed the steamer (or she passed us would, perhaps, be the most correct way of putting it) about half a way to Gualeguaychu, and our little craft sailed up to the pier, about the middle of the afternoon; and before I had gone more than a few steps from the shore, I met the friend whom I had come so far to join. After the natural greetings and enquiries after relations and friends, we went together to the hotel, and I found that Frank had brought in a horse for me to ride out with him to the place where he was living, which was about five leagues from Gualeguaychu; a league in South America (I may as well here say) is a little over three miles. We were detained a day or two in the town, as I was obliged to wait for my luggage, and to pass it through the custom-house, always a tiresome business, and particularly so in this country, as the duty is heavy on various articles indispensable to all emigrants.

Gualeguaychu, where I now found myself landed, was then a superior place to Fray Bentos, with good accommodation, and fair shops; and many English having settled in its neighbourhood, some of them may generally be found in the town, where they meet for business, to fetch their letters, obtain stores, and for the same inscrutable reasons which collect all the farmers in a country neighbourhood in England once a week in their own little market town, whether they have anything to do there or not. Here I first made acquaintance with some real settlers, compared the accounts of their various failures or successes, and formed some idea of my future mode of life. After a few days we rode out to my friend's home, which was only fifteen miles distant, and rejoiced in the picturesque name of Santa Barbara. It was rather an original residence, built entirely of fine reeds, the roof and walls just alike; in fact, the thing it most resembled was a straw rick with the inside hollowed out. This little nest, the work of Frank's own hands, contained a bedroom and sitting room, the latter possessing a stove.

He bad been sharing these extensive accommodations with one companion, an elderly man, an amphibious sort of creature, of uncertain position and doubtful nationality, one of those people occasionally to be met with about the world who belong to nowhere in particular. He had, I think, originally been a Dane. He left a few days after my arrival, being of no further use at the establishment; nor is it, I hope, unkind to say that, from the size of our mansion, his room was much more valuable than his company.

Frank's was a sheep farm; he rented three thousand acres, i.e. about half a league; his stock was two thousand sheep, and in twelve months the flock had nearly doubled itself. Entre Rios is the favourite part of the Republic, but as it has been settled for more than ten years (by the English, that is to say -the date of the discovery by the Spaniards was somewhat earlier), land is not to be had without a considerable outlay. It has decided attractions, as, besides the pleasantness of the country, with its hills, woods, and abundant streams, most of the inhabitants are the sons of English gentlemen. Some of the older settlers have made for themselves comfortable quarters, and their estancias are not without the home look that the English delight to carry with them all over the world; the only nation that approach them in this respect, so far as my experience goes, being the Germans. This was, of course, especially the case where the influence of a lady prevailed, and there are some very happy English families to be found in Entre Rios. No lady, however, had better venture to undertake the life unless she has a good health, a brave heart, and an active pair of hands, for all will be wanted. B., a neighbour of ours, had a wife who fulfilled all these conditions. She had been one of the prettiest and most fashionable young ladies in Dublin, but that did not prevent her from cooking, washing, and doing the work of the house, whenever, as was not seldom the case, the servants failed; and I hope I may be allowed to add, that she looked as pretty and as happy while engaged in these occupations, as by all accounts she did in her former way of life. Some ladies have still harder work, as I know of one who kept her husband's sheep, but I sincerely trust these animals will in the end prove lucrative enough to keep her in the comfort she well deserves; at present I fear she, like myself, is a little inclined to consider sheep-farming a delusion and a snare. Looking after the sheep was my own occupation when first I arrived. Frank milked the cows, being the most expert hand at that business. He also cooked our dinner, while I was scullerymaid, and washed up the things, but before long I graduated in the noble and useful art myself. The straw house proved fairly comfortable after the first awful night, when I might as well have slept in a henhouse for all the rest I had; but either the fleas tired of me or I got used to them, for I never suffered afterwards.

As this was not to be our permanent home I did not feel obliged to stick very closely to work, and partly employed myself in riding about the country, and making acquaintance with the owners of the various estancias, whom I found a very hospitable set. We had a little duck-shooting in the neighbouring streams. Shooting is the sport of the country, unless you have a fancy for stalking ostriches, of which in this part there are great numbers. They are not so large as the African species, nor are their feathers in equal request in the London shops; but they are nevertheless of considerable value, and a good deal of money may be made by the skilful hunter.

The first sight of them was one of the things which made me realise that I was far away from Europe and the old familiar creatures; and very curious were my sensations when, a few days after my arrival, I sat down to write my first letters home. Frank had gone to a neighbour to assist him in the interesting occupation of parting his flock, and I was left quite alone to look after the house and sheep. I seated myself near the door of our little hut, and having arranged a somewhat rude desk, looked out at the scene I was about to endeavour to describe. The slightly undulating green plain, covered with long rough grass, stretched away to an interminable distance, a few patches of red and purple verbenas making a slight variation of tint here and there in the long waves of verdure; some little way from the road a number of ostriches strolled about, with majestic indifference to my presence, though I must say that some natural instinct inspired them with the unhappy idea of keeping just out of gunshot. A pet lamb was strolling in and out of the house as contentedly as the pig in an Irish cabin; and I could contemplate my sheep - or, to speak more correctly, Frank's - browsing in the distance. I was occasionally obliged to pursue these fugitive animals, whose rapid movements would make an English sheep stare. In all countries sheep move along as they feed, more rapidly than those who have not studied their habits might suppose, but in South America they become so active from being quite unrestrained by hedges, that their usual pace is about four miles an hour; and it call be so rapid when anything alarms them, that I well remember once riding after a flock of sheep, who went so fast for nearly five leagues (sixteen or seventeen miles), that it was all I could do to keep up with them at a gallop. Frank's flock were not quite so active as this, and I had plenty of horses to pursue them with, as Frank possessed a tropilla of sixteen steeds; so we were well mounted. Mingled with the bleating of the sheep came the less pleasing hum of insects. A large colony of wasps had established themselves at the end of our house; and as the wasps in this country are about two inches long and sting in proportion, they are by no means agreeable companions. Ants of a colossal size were running over everything; and spiders, large, hairy, and black, about the size of one's hand, might be seen by anyone curious in investigating dark corners; indeed, the insects of South America are among its greatest wonders.

But animal and insect life were the only varieties in the monotonous scene before me, and the utter absence of all human sounds on one's spirits at first, with the feeling of a painful blank. As I took out the letters I had to answer, and read all the little particulars of English home life, the contrast between the well-remembered house and garden that rose up before my imagination, and the wide green camp that lay stretched before my eyes, was vivid enough to bring with it reflections that every Englishman who has been in the same situation will well understand.

I was soon obliged to rouse myself from these sentimental meditations by the necessity of preparing my dinner, in case I wished to partake of any food that day. Our meals consisted generally of mutton and hard biscuits, which were washed down by a draught from the river. This was occasionally mixed with caña, the chief drink of the country. Caña is a kind of white rum made in Brazil, and is excessively cheap, too much so, indeed, for the good of many of the inhabitants, and it is much to be wished that some beverage answering to beer or cider could be introduced. The other favourite drink of the country, mate, is free from the objections that may be raised against caña. It is made from a plant called yerba mate, which grows in Paraguay and Brazil, and is, I believe (for I have never seen it), a small shrub, the leaves and stalks of which are dried and then used much in the same manner as tea, being put with boiling water into a small pot made out of a gourd; but, instead of being poured into cups when the mate is served, each of the company sucks it up through a reed or silver tube, called a bombilla. Milk and sugar are sometimes added, and it then becomes a very agreeable beverage. I thought mate a very hot and bitter drink at first, but I have now become extremely fond of it.

A short time after this day of solitude Frank and I were both invited to help a neighbour part his sheep; so, committing our own flock to the care of a casual assistant, we both went over to Mr. C.'s estancia, which was about a league from ours. It was a long low house, built of bricks and thatched with paja, the same material of which our own abode was constructed. Paja is a kind of reed, which grows in great abundance by the river. Mr. C. had been about sixteen years in the country, and was getting on very fairly; he had begun without any capital, and was now the owner of a flock of sheep which in England would be considered enormous. These animals we now proceeded to part, as it is called, which was a work of some difficulty. There are no fences or hedges in Entre Rios, so that sheep can only be kept in separate flocks in the daytime by some one watching each division when they are feeding on the plains. At night they are driven into small pens made of posts and wire, and called corrals. The shepherd is almost always on horseback by day, as that is the most convenient way of watching his restless flock. After our labours were concluded we were sumptuously entertained by Mr. C, and introduced to his wife and children; the two youngest boys were born in Entre Rios, and had become thorough little Gauchos; though only about ten and twelve, they could ride beautifully an almost any horse, an used to climb up like monkeys, putting one little bare foot on the horse's knee, and then by means of the mane swinging themselves up on its back, where they rode without any saddle, and sometimes, for a change, with their faces to the tail. I made great friends with these young gentlemen, and they often paid me visits and bathed with me, being as skilful at swimming as at riding. Their education was not very advanced in the arts of civilisation, but they were very amusing companions. Our life in Entre Rios was much of this kind, during the short time I remained at Santa Barbara; it was varied by visits to the neighbours, kind hospitalities received from them, and the care of our own little property; but this peaceful sort of life did not last long, for, after much discussion of our prospects, Frank and I came to the conclusion that we must pitch our tent elsewhere. Entre Rios was already over-civilised and over-peopled, to suit our ideas. The piece of land we now occupied would soon be too small for our increasing flocks, and no more was to be procured in the neighbourhood. Two friends of Frank's, who, like ourselves, had come out with the intention of sheep-farming, had begun by travelling all over the Argentine Republic before deciding where they could commence operations with the best prospect of success. They had now settled in the province of Cordoba, near Frayle Muerto, and their report of the country disposed us to follow their example.

CHAPTER III

SEARCH FOR OTHER CAMP – ROSARIO - THE DILIGENCE - FRAYLE MUERTO - FIND FELLOW-COUNTRYMEN - EXPLORE THE VACANT CAMP – PROVINCE OF CORDOBA - RIDE TO THE CITY OF CORDOBA - WOODS OF THE COUNTRY - NATIVE WAGGONS, ETC. – CORDOBA - THE SIERRAS - BUY CAMP, AND RETURN TO VIEW IT.

It was early in May that we started on our expedition of discovery. We descended the Uruguay to Buenos Ayres, and after a few days there, started off for Rosario and Frayle Muerto. The chief highways of the Plate country are the rivers, and we now embarked for Rosario on the Parana, the river that bounds the western side of Entre Rios. The scenery resembles that of the Uruguay, as we were again ascending a stream of about twenty miles in breadth, studded with many islands which interrupt the view from bank to bank, causing it to present the appearance of a lake rather than of a river. No great beauty enlivens the scene between Buenos Ayres and Rosario, as the flattish land on either side the Parana is scantily wooded, and no hills occur to vary its monotony. The steamers are fairly comfortable, and ply only for passenger traffic; heavy goods coming up and down in sailing vessels. The voyage of two hundred and fifty miles was performed in about twenty-four hours, and on landing we repaired to the Hôtel de Colon.

The weather was beginning to become wintry, as May in the River Plate answers very much to our November. I had not had any experience of the height of summer as yet, being only arrived in March, when the temperature is much the same as that of an English August. We spent about a fortnight in Rosario, and made constant expeditions to the neighbouring camps, but none of them suited our ideas; there were a good many reasons against them, but the important one was, that so near a large town land was too expensive for our finances.

So we resolved to become the pioneers of civilisation, and to go on to Frayle Muerto. Rosario stands on the high banks of the river, in the middle of a perfectly flat green plain, but the river makes some variety in the view. It is a rapidly increasing place, at present containing about sixty thousand people, and, being quite a modern town, is much better built than Buenos Ayres, whose narrow streets, from the plan of which that town is built, cannot possibly be widened. The port of Rosario is very good, and quite large ships can come close in. This is a great advantage to settlers in the province of Cordoba, as in this way things can be sent direct by water from England to Rosario. There are a great many English settlers round Rosario, and a little later than the time of which I am now writing, one was always sure, in coming down to Rosario, to find some English friends, either at the hotel or in the English stores. Rosario will shortly be lighted with gas, like any town in the old country. Common oil lamps had been introduced for some little time when I was first there; but before that a very primitive sort of light was used in the shape of potro oil, that is to say, oil made from mares fat; potro means a colt. There is now a railway from Rosario to Cordoba, called the Central Argentine, opened as far as Villa Nueva, that is, for about two hundred miles, and the whole will soon be finished. The flat nature of the country makes it very suitable for railways, as scarcely anything in the shape of cuttings or embankments are required; tunnels are quite unknown; and the bridges over the rivers are the only part of the railways that need any time to make. The railways are made entirely by English contractors, and pay everyone concerned in them extremely well. A new one from Buenos Ayres, to Mendoza is talked of, and will in all probability be shortly begun, and if it reaches Mendoza, will no doubt be continued through the Andes to Chili. In fact, the River Plate ought to be one of the most flourishing countries in the world, from its great natural advantages of every sort; and the settlers there would appear unable to avoid shortly becoming millionaires.

As soon as Frank and I had decided that the Rosario camps were too expensive for us, we resolved to try those round Frayle Muerto, and accordingly took our places in the diligence, the railway being then only open for a few miles. A diligence is never a very delightful mode of travelling; and the South American diligence is perhaps as uncomfortable a conveyance as any known. It is pulled along by from six or eight horses, according to the state of the roads; a man rides on each of these animals, who pull from the girths, and proceed at full gallop, without the least regard to ruts, biscacha holes, &c. The South American roads are not macadamised, being nothing in fact but a track over the prairie. About six unfortunate beings are able to go inside this machine, which looks rather like an aged-coach, and two more can sit in front with the driver. We provided ourselves with various necessaries for travelling, among which were several pistols, by no means the least important part of the outfit. We left Rosario early one morning, and reached Frayle Muerto on the evening of the second day; staying by the way at a small post-house. The diligence changes horses about every four leagues. The accommodations at the post-houses are not very splendid, the beds consisting of our own rugs on the floor; and our dinner or supper was usually walking happily about when arrived, and not therefore remarkably tender when it appeared on the table. The country through which we passed was, as usual, perfectly flat, with only a few occasional bushes or a rancho, that is to say, a mud hut, to be seen; a few deer and ostriches sometimes appeared, but the most frequent objects were the large hawks called coranchos, who were generally engaged in picking the bones of some dead animal; they are much hated by the sheep farmer, as they take every opportunity of killing his young lambs, by picking out their eyes. As we got near Frayle Muerto some of the passengers began to exhibit signs of uneasiness about the Indians; and the agreeable idea dawned upon us, that the inhabitants of this part of the country live in the same sort of general expectation of a sudden attack from those delightful neighbours, as the visitors round Vesuvius do of an eruption from the burning mountain; and, though I did not believe it at the time, I must say that experience has taught me that their fears are by no means unfounded. We were "quitte pour la peur", however, on this occasion, but did not get to Frayle Muerto till it was too dark to see what the place was like. The proper name is San Geronimo, but it is always called Frayle Muerto, which means the "Dead Friar", from a tradition of some priest having been murdered there. We slept at the post-house in the usual uncomfortable way, and the next morning, finding there was no breakfast to be had, we went out in a search of some, and bought some bread and sardines, which we ate by the river side. After this frugal meal we strolled about the town a little; it was a poor place, very few decent houses, and most of the streets composed of mud ranchos. Our first object was to get some horses; and while walking about in rather a forlorn way we suddenly met two Scotchmen, who had just settled about four leagues out of the town. They gave us a kind welcome to Frayle Muerto, and assisted us in getting two horses to ride out with them to their estancia, which was only three miles from the house of the friends Frank had come up to see.

We got out to Arbol Chato about dark, and found the house consisted of only one room, as B., the owner of the place, had been there but a short time; the kind welcome, however, which we received made up for any deficiency in the accommodations. B. was a sheep farmer like everyone else, and a long talk after dinner about the prospects of the country and the camps near Frayle Muerto encouraged us to think we had found the right spot to settle in.

Next morning we rode over to Los Algarobitas, where Frank's friends were settled. Their accommodation was much the same as B.'s - one small room with a ditch round it, as a defence against the much-dreaded Indians; but at that time none of us at all believed in the danger. P., K., and P. were all Scotchmen, and had only been a few months in this part of the country, of which they also thought very well. We stayed with them about a week, during which time Frank and I, with two of our friends, accompanied by a native acting as vaqueano, or guide, made a small expedition to the south, to look at the camps there. As we went over a large district of land we were forced to camp out at night, and found for the first evening a pleasant spot under some trees, where we settled ourselves pretty comfortably. We fell in with some wild cattle, one of which we killed for our evening repast. There are a good many of these sort of wandering animals about who have been carried off by the Indians and then escaped, and of course anyone who can catch them is free to do so. The vaqueano effected this with a lasso, and we then shot our prisoner and proceeded to skin him; and after a delicious supper followed by some pipes, we retired to our rugs, and slept very soundly rolled up in them; though I woke in rather a freezing condition, as long wet boots are not very agreeable to sleep in on a winter's night.

The province of Cordoba in which we now were is one of the largest in the Republic, and runs down to the south-east to the province of Buenos Ayres, touching the provinces of San Louis and San Juan to the west. The southern part of Cordoba forms therefore part of the frontier of the Republic. My readers must excuse these geographical disquisitions; but since my return to England I have been led to think that South American geography is not much understood by those who have no reason for taking a personal interest in the subject; indeed, various intelligent people with whom I have conversed evidently overlook the existence of two continents in the New World altogether, and consider me to be residing in a remote part of the Southern States, for I am constantly asked how the civil war has affected me. I hope therefore that, with the help of an ordinary map of South America, to which I must refer my readers, I have made my position tolerably clear to them, and that they understand we were now in the south-eastern part of the province of Cordoba, and about twenty leagues from the frontier, which is supposed to divide the Republic from de Indian territory. There are a few forts scattered alone the boundary, but at present they are scarcely of any use in keeping out the Indians. The whole of the country we were now exploring was to the south of Frayle Muerto, and quite uninhabited, and stretched down to a region as little known as the desert of Sahara. The province of Cordoba has long been terribly exposed to Indian incursions, but just round Rosario the settlers are, comparatively speaking safe; and I hope in time, as they become more inhabited, the camps round Frayle Muerto will be equally free from these invaders. I ought, perhaps, just to explain here the word "camp", which I have so often used; it simply means "the country", as distinguished from "the town", and is the abbreviation of the Spanish word campo; and when one talks of being out in the camp it answers a good deal to the Australian expression of "out in the bush". The Frayle Muerto camps are well watered, and the pasture is excellent for cattle, especially that part of the land which runs down to the river Saladillo, which rises some forty leagues from Frayle Muerto, and runs into the Rio Tercero close to a small village from which it takes the name of Saladillo. All the land round Frayle Muerto is marked out by the Government of the province of Cordoba into lots of from two to four square leagues in extent, and is sold by auction in Cordoba. A square league contains rather over six thousand acres to one lot or "suerte" as it is called, and makes a very fair sized run. As an auction was just advertised to come off, and some of the land on the southern bank of the Saladillo, and distant about eleven leagues from Frayle Muerto, was to be put up for sale, we determined to start for Cordoba, and, if it went it a reasonable price, to become the purchasers of this suerte, as of course it is a great object to be near permanent water.

We accordingly bade good-bye to our friends, and started for Cordoba, on horseback, preferring even the post-horses, bad as they were, to the still more uncomfortable diligence. This mode of travelling is cheaper than by diligence, costing only about a penny a mile; and as we rode behind the diligence we always found horses ready whenever we got to a post-house.

The conductor of the diligence was the same with whom we had came up from Rosario to Frayle Muerto, and as he very civilly offered to take our saddle-bags and rugs, our horses were not encumbered with any extra weight. Our road from Frayle Muerto to Cordoba lay nearly the whole of the way through wood, or monte, as it is there called, and was certainly more picturesque than the parts between Rosario and Frayle Muerto. The trees that enclose the road are chiefly algaroba, chañar, espinilla and tala, all thorny, and none of them growing to a great height. The algaroba is a very hard wood, and makes capital posts and firewood, being very easily split, and it has rather a pleasant smell when cut open. It is a sort of reddish colour inside, a little like cedar, and has a pretty grain when polished, and makes very nice furniture. The leaf is long and feathery, and it bears every third year a yellow fruit like a long beanpod in shape, with very hard seeds inside. The pod has a very pleasant sweet taste, and horses and cattle are exceedingly fond of it.

The chañar has a smooth yellow bark and very pretty yellow flower, with a little fruit something like a medlar in taste. The wood is exceedingly tough, and very useful for axe-handles, shafts, &c. These, with the quebracho, of which there are two or three sorts, and the nandubay, which grows in great abundance in Entre Rios and parts of Santa Fe, are the chief woods of the country. The nandubay is very hard, and will last in the ground for an almost endless time, as there are corrals standing that are known to be more than a hundred years old made of nandubay posts. The quebracho colorado, which grows in great abundance beyond Cordoba, is very useful for making the heavy native bullock-carts, which are very clumsy affairs. They are made without any iron at all, and are covered with a sort of little hut, called a tolda, made of bent sticks thatched and covered at the top with hides stretched over them. The whole of the produce of the upper provinces is brought down either in these conveyances or on the backs of mules; and it is very curious at first to see the long strings of these carts creeping slowly along with six bullocks to each, with their wheels creaking so fearfully that they can be heard a very long way off, for the natives think that the creaking of the wheels makes the bullocks go better, and so never take the trouble to grease them. Driving a bullock-cart seems to suit the natives capitally, as they can sit quietly in the cart, and smoke their endless cigarettes, and shout at the bullocks to their hearts' content. Some of the journeys must be rather tedious, I should think, as they sometimes last for more than three months.

The ore from the mines of San Juan is chiefly brought down on the backs of mules, large troops of which may constantly be seen passing through Frayle Muerto. They carry a tremendous weight on their backs, and bring down, besides the silver and copper ore, large boxes of raisins, barrels of sugar, dried fruit, and rolls of tobacco, and carry up, on their return journey, flour, yerba, &c. They always follow a bell-mare, which is led by a man in advance, and the drivers bring up the rear; rough-looking fellows in thick ponchos, and always wearing immense iron spurs, weighing perhaps a couple of pounds each. But to return to our journey. We had to cross the Rio Tercero at Villa Nueva, a small town about seventeen leagues from Frayle Muerto, and thirty-three from Cordoba. It was then a poor place, but since the railway has reached it it has greatly increased, and will some day probably become rather important. The road from Frayle Muerto to Villa Nueva is very pretty in places, as one can here and there catch a glimpse of the Rio Tercero, with its high banks covered with weeping willows and dense wood filled with creepers; and to make a progress through these woods, except where there is a road, is extremely laborious. The Rio Segundo, which we crossed about eight leagues from Cordoba, is very much of the same nature as the Tercero, with high banks and sandy bottom, generally very shallow, but after heavy rains becoming a perfect torrent, filled up to the top of the banks eighteen and twenty feet in depth, carrying large trees along with the current. This river is the chief obstacle on the Central Argentine Railway, but the bridge across it, about eleven hundred feet in length, has been successfully accomplished.

We passed two nights at post-houses between Frayle Muerto and Cordoba, and reached that town on the morning of the second day. The sierras of Cordoba can be seen for a very long distance, and look very refreshing after so much flat country. Approaching Cordoba, one travels through several miles of thick wood; and nothing can be seen of the town until you come right above it, as it lies down in a sort of hole with hills on all sides. The view as one comes down into the town is really very pretty, as there are some very fine buildings in Cordoba, and several churches, besides the cathedral, and a large Jesuit college, to which the Jesuits have now returned for at one time nearly all the town and most of the land around belonged to them; but they were all turned out, and have only been allowed to come back within the last few years. We had a letter of introduction to Mr. T., almost the only Englishman at that time in Cordoba, and we luckily fell in with him directly we arrived, as he had come to hear the news by the diligence. He advised us to stay at the Hôtel de Paris, kept by a Frenchman and his wife, where we were very comfortable. This hotel looks out into the large Plaza, which used to be very gay in the evenings, as the people came and walked there to hear the band play.

Mr. T. kindly told us everything he could about the sales of land, one of which was coming off two days after our arrival. He also told us of what sounded a good speculation, namely, a place that was to be sold in the sierra about ten leagues from Cordoba, where cattle might be fed for the market. There are some very fine old places in the sierras, most of which have belonged to the Jesuits, but they have fallen a great deal out of repair, and one of these was now for sale. T. wished to buy it, but had not quite capital enough; and so asked us if we felt inclined to join him in the speculation. Frank accordingly determined to ride out and see this place, while I remained in Cordoba for the sale, meaning to purchase the piece of land on the banks of the Saladillo if it did not fetch a very high price. T. came with me on the morning of the sale, which took place just in front of the cabildo or sort of justice hall of the town. Two or three other lots were put up before ours, which were knocked down without much opposition, as there were very few bidders; and we got ours, four square leagues in quantity, at about sixpence an acre, which we could hardly consider very dear.

Frank returned from his expedition in a day or two, very much struck with the beauty of the sierras, but he did not consider it worth our while to think further of the place that he had been to see. It was a very pretty picturesque spot, and the buildings of stone (of which there is plenty to be got up in the sierras, although there is not a vestige of one in the pampas) had once been very good, but had fallen so out of repair that it would have involved a considerable outlay to make them habitable. There was an old chapel built by the Jesuits, but now used as a shed, and the fences of the orchards and paddocks of alfalfa or lucerne wanted a great deal doing to them to make them good. The great advantage in the place was a charming stream, which was never dry; and if we had taken the place, our business would have been to grow alfalfa to fatten cattle for the Cordoba market. All the alfalfa and other crops round the town are irrigated by streams from the sierras, as in the winter it never rains in Cordoba; and so, if it were not for the irrigation, the cattle would all die. The feeding business is therefore profitable; as fat animals for the market, which in the summer are worth perhaps 20 Bolivian dollars (about 3l.), are in the winter worth 10l., and sometimes 12l. However, we considered that as so much would have to be done to the place in the way of repairing the buildings, making new fences, and putting the channels for irrigating the alfalfa to rights, we had better give up that idea and try our luck in the Pampas in our newly-bought land.

We accordingly left Cordoba and rode down again to Frayle Muerto, where we spent a few days with our kind friends at the Algarobitas; and while there we rode out to inspect our new property, which as yet we had not actually visited. A German, who imagined he knew these parts, offered to act as guide, but the day being misty and our leader's ideas of the way extremely vague, we wandered about for a long time, and finding we could not hit off the right place that day, we passed the night under the shelter of some small bushes. By the next morning, the fog had cleared off, and about the middle of the day we reached the Saladillo, the boundary on one side of our property. Our estate was on the opposite side of the river from the Algarobitas, from which it was really only twenty miles distant, but we found, to our chagrin, on reaching the bank, that the river was too much swollen by rain for us to attempt crossing on horse-back; and as the weather was much too cool for swimming to be pleasant, we could only contemplate our future paradise from the opposite shore, our minds clearly opening to the agreeable fact that we were destined to be the first English residents between (this part of) the Saladillo and Patagonia, or I might say, Cape Horn. Pondering these things, and admiring the arrangements of fortune, we were pleased at perceiving that the river was covered with waterfowl of all descriptions - swans, geese, ducks, flamingoes, stork, &c., which gave hopes of abundant future dinners to the new lords of the soil. We remarked also, with some joy, two or three trees in the distance on our estate, which was of course as flat as all the rest of the country; it looked very green and fertile, however, and the herbage close to the river was a sort of rich clover, which promised well for pasture. When we had looked as long as we cared, we rode off, and after more wandering about, and a very cold night out of doors, as it was freezing hard, we returned to the Algarobitas.

CHAPTER IV

PREPARE TO SETTLE ON OUR CAMP - CASA DE FIERRO - JOURNEY FROM ROSARIO - RECRUITS - OUR FIRST MEAL ON OUR OWN ESTATE - WELL-DIGGING - DOMESTIC ARRANGEMENTS - CORRALS - MORALS OF NATIVE SERVANTS - OUR FIRST CHRISTMAS IN THE CAMP - ENDEAVOUR TO PURCHASE SHEEP.

We now set seriously to work to conclude the purchase of our land, having quite determined to settle near Frayle Muerto. The possibility of Indian depredations was the only drawback; but these were represented to us by the people in authority, both at Rosario and Cordoba, as a trifling risk. We were about three hundred miles from the Indian settlements, and were told that they had the greatest dread of fire-arms, and never would dream of attacking well-armed Englishmen in a property-built house, but merely scoured the country at one time of year in quest of any stray horses and cattle they could pick up; sheep they were said never to touch, as they could not drive them fast enough to keep up with their own rapid pace; in short, they were represented to us more as the kind of pest gipsies might be in a lonely English neighbourhood than a serious danger; and it was under this belief that we bought our land and determined to settle so far south. We also expected fully, at this time, that the land around us would have been quickly bought up, and that the Government would protect us; the Paraguayan war, and a very sad event which I shall relate by and by, were the two things most against us, and for these unforeseen hindrances, I am convinced our choice of land would have proved already, as I hope it will eventually prove, a wise one.

There was at this time no bank in Cordoba, so I was forced to journey down to Buenos Ayres in search of our money, which I then took up to Cordoba, intending to return with my title-deeds; but lawyers are as slow at their work here as in any other part of the world, and, after waiting some time, I was it last obliged to come away without the deeds, my friend T.

undertaking to send them down to us. Frank in the meantime went off to Entre Rios to collect our scattered goods. We next met in Rosario, when I found that he had made an important purchase in Buenos Ayres, which was neither more nor less than a small iron dwelling-house. He had come across an energetic speculator, who had just imported several of these articles of different sizes and prices. Ours cost about 80l., and though not the most comfortable residence in the world - as every change in the weather, either of heat or cold, was instantly felt, until we might almost as well have been thermometers - it was, on the whole, very useful. It excited a great sensation in Frayle Muerto, where we were known as "the owners of the iron house", and regarded with great respect; and as one of us passed in the street the enquiry as to who we were was usually answered, "El dueño de la casa de fierro"; to which the admiring populace would reply, "que hombre".

During our short stay in Rosario we fell in with three young Englishmen, who became afterwards some of our greatest friends; two of them, indeed, who were brothers, Charlie and Gerald T., lived with us for many months, and bought the land adjoining ours. The other, K., purchased land nearer to Rosario, in the province of Santa Fe, and was soon joined there by two brother officers; and their estancia of Las Rosas is now about the best in that province, and well known to all their friends for its pleasant hospitality. We afterwards became very well acquainted with K., but did not see much more of him at this time, as he determined to remain near Rosario; while the T.s, who had been travelling for about a year in search of a spot to settle in, having found nothing yet that they liked, resolved, on hearing of our new purchase and determination, to settle in an untried region, to accompany us, and see whether our part of the country might not also suit their ideas. My spirits were much raised by meeting with the T.s, one of whom I had slightly known in England. Both brothers had been in the army, but had sold out on hearing of the rapid fortunes which might be amassed in South America. We resolved at once to go to our property, and commence our great start in life; and, therefore, set to work to collect house-hold goods. We procured pots and pans and other domestic articles, purchased a cart and ten horses, a small tent, and numerous stores, and started off, riding and driving. The party consisted of Frank and myself, Charlie and Gerald T., and an Englishman, called Henry, whom we had hired to cook for us. He was a clever man, who had seen better days, and might have done well if he had been less fond of roving about; he had travelled in India, and been lately in Brazil, engaged in making one of the railways there; originally, I believe, he had been in the English navy. He was a most excellent cook, and a very useful assistant from his travelling experiences, and used to light our fires, pitch the tent, and make everything comfortable for us at night, while we were doing the same good offices for our horses.

We guided our course by the line of railway, which was marked out for about sixty miles, and then struck into the posting track. We took about ten days on this expedition, pasture being scarce and the water very salt and bad, so that our horses could not travel very fast. We reached the Rio Carcarañal on the third day, and found there was no way of crossing the river except by a ford, near which a railway-bridge was being constructed. The water was rather deep and muddy, and about the middle of the river our heavily-laden cart stuck fast, and refused to move. There was a railway encampment on the other side, and about one hundred natives who were employed on the railway collected on the half-finished bridge, and jeered at our misfortune. We toiled at our unfortunate cart, endeavouring to drag it out with lassos, with feelings of rage at the amused spectators; but we were at length reduced to hiring four or five of them, who at last succeeded in dragging our property ashore. We found some English engineers at the encampment, and were hospitably entertained by them. No other event occurred worth recording, and we reached Frayle Muerto safely, and encamped in the wood near it, in a very pleasant spot close to the river, where we rested ourselves, and our horses, passing our time in shooting and bathing, and otherwise enjoying ourselves.

After two days' rest the caravan moved on, our train being augmented by two new followers: one was an Irishman, named Jack, who was engaged to dig our well, and the large ditch supposed to be necessary for a defence; the other was a native, named Lisada, rather clever, but not bearing a high character, and who preferred racing and gambling to manual labour. Our reason for engaged him, notwithstanding these defects, was a very simple one, viz. that he was almost the only native who had the courage to come so far south with us, the Gauchos being all terribly afraid of the Indians. Jack also was willing to risk it; and we started with these valiant companions, having engaged to pay Lisada about 2l. a month and to keep him besides.

Jack was paid for his work in the same sort of proportion. Wages are enormously high, and one of the great drains on the settler's purse. Lisada, to do him justice, was fairly brave, but Jack's courage did not prove of a high order. We slept two nights on our way, and reached the banks of the Saladillo on the evening of the 7th of October. The next morning - after sticking once or twice in the river and various other little accidents, such as Lisada's girths breaking, when he fell into the water and was fished out, amid shouts of laughter - we all reached the opposite bank, and stood upon our own property. The river was rather low upon this occasion, being only about two hundred and forty feet across, but when well filled it is about three or four hundred yards in width. The banks are very low, and a great part of the stream is shallow, but in the middle of the river the horses generally have to swim about fifty or sixty yards; we were very lucky in finding the river so low, as we were able to get our cart across. The passage being effected, we rode up to look at the trees, which were about a mile from the river, and as we approached them a small lioncub rushed out from some low bushes near. He was soon caught by the dogs, and, having been killed, we thought, as we were very short of meat, we would try how he tasted; and, having roasted him in his skin - a favourite mode of cooking in South America, called "carne con cuero" - we breakfasted on lion for the first time, and found it very good.

Lisada told us that the small group of quebracho trees under which we were now standing was a sort of land-mark to travellers in the camp, and known as Monte Molino, so we resolved to call our estancia by that name.

After breakfast, as we were prowling about our new domain, the dogs suddenly became again extremely excited, and the cause of their agitation was soon apparent, as a large lioness rushed out of the bushes, and took shelter under a thick tree with branches down to the ground. The dogs were afraid to attack her, and several revolver shots having been fired without much effect, I ran to the encampment for my rifle, and putting a bullet through her head the engagement was soon ended. We kept the skin as a trophy of our exploit. The other cub emerged from a hole some days after, looking very thin and wretched, and was killed by the dogs.

We soon decided that our house should be built among the trees; and having pitched our little tent there, proceeded to make ourselves as comfortable as circumstances would allow.

Jack began his labours on the well, selecting a spot close to the house which he thought promising. We had brought a large hide bucket and pulley, with which we dragged the earth out, working it by a horse. After five days' hard digging we came to water at the depth of about thirty feet. At the cry of "agua" we all rushed up in a state of delight, and found our labours were rewarded by all abundant supply of water, so extremely salt that it was almost impossible to drink it, and for the short time we were obliged to do so it made us quite ill. We were obliged to begin a new well nearly a mile from the house, and chose a spot in a hollow near a small laguna. This second well turned out very drinkable, though, of course, the necessity of bringing up water from a mile off every day was an immense trouble.

The water in wells on the higher ground is, as a rule, almost always salt, while down in the little valleys the supply of water is generally good. The salt comes, I believe, from the great quantity of saltpetre in the soil through which the water drains, the wells being of course supplied not from real springs but from land-soaks. Why there is less salt on the lower ground I am not enough of a geologist to say, but all the water in the Pampas is slightly impregnated with it, and would, I think, always taste slightly brackish to a new comer, though to us our second well appeared very fresh and good. The mouth of a well which has been used for some time always looks white, from the salt which has been left there from the water spilt on the ground, and when our river was low the banks looked as if covered with a slight fall of snow.

Our first well was rather a nuisance, as we were too busy or too lazy to fill it up for some time, and a pitfall close to your house, some six feet across and thirty feet deep, is rather inconvenient. Some unlucky stray animals went down it once or twice; one of our horses fell into it on one occasion, and as all our lassos were away, the bullock-carts being sent for something to a distance, he was forced to remain two or three days at the bottom of the well before we could drag him out. We threw him down grass, and, like poor "Ophelia", he had "too much of water", though he did not share her fate, as he was drawn up triumphantly, still living: but after about three days he died. He must have had a very unpleasant time of it, poor fellow, as his tail was quite full of frogs.

After two or three days of well-digging Frank and the two T.s started off on horseback for Rosario, Frank intending to meet his youngest brother, who had just come out from England to join us, and at the same time to bring up our property, including the iron house, in our bullock-wagons.

We were much delighted at the two T.s having decided to purchase the next piece of land to ours, to which they at once took a fancy; the prospect of being such near neighbours was very pleasant to us all, and the reality was, if possible, still more pleasant as long as it lasted,

which, to our mutual regret, was not so long as we had hoped. The two brothers went off now to Cordoba, to arrange the purchase and collect their various possessions, while I was left with my three companions, Henry, Jack, and Lisada, to complete the well and begin our ditch.

In order to keep up discipline in the establishment I slept in the tent, while my domestics bivouacked outside, Henry making himself very comfortable in a hammock in one of the quebracho trees, Lisada, and Jack on the ground beneath him. We kept no watch at night, and took our chance of Indians. We depended on our guns and dogs for our dinner, and once or twice captured a stray cow. The men worked well, and we had traced out the ditch, which enclosed a space of fifty yards square, and was intended to be about six feet deep and six broad, when, after ten days' absence, I was very glad to welcome Frank and his young brother. They had ridden up from Rosario, and came out from the village of Saladillo in pouring rain, which was so violent that they found us all huddled into the tent, as the only place of shelter. It was rather a dismal welcome for G., who had come out from England on the strength of descriptions sent home of the delights of life in the Pampas, and he looked a little blank at the first sight of his future habitation. A good dinner of wild ducks was prepared in honour of his arrival, and when this had been discussed he took a more cheerful view of his prospects.

Frank had seen our goods off from Rosario before he left it himself, and about two days after his arrival we beheld a joyful sight in the shape of the bullock-carts slowly approaching. They of course all stuck fast in the river, and were only rescued after several hours' severe work; but we got everything safely up to the encampment that night, and next morning begin to put up our house. It was a delightful moment when this was concluded after two days' hard work, and we had again a roof over our heads of something thicker than canvas. We had two rooms in our iron dwelling, each twelve feet square, and had brought up some stools and tables to furnish them with; these, with our beds, washing-stands, two chests of drawers, and an arm-chair, gave the place a very comfortable look; and with some boards which we had brought up from Rosario we soon knocked up a small kitchen at one end of the house, where Henry began his culinary operations.

The feelings of civilised life so far prevailed in the camp that our domestic arrangements led to the first unpleasantness in our little colony. Henry, after waiting on us, was in the habit of taking his own meals quietly at a side table in the house when we had finished, first supplying Jack and Lisada, who were not invited to join us in our repast, with their rations in the tent, where all the servants now slept. Jack's dignity was unable to stand this supposed slight, and he accordingly left us, in spite of all we could say to mollify him, assigning this as the reason of his departure. Lisada, whose feelings were less sensitive, was then left to his solitary meals, and his appetite seemed no way affected by his companion's departure. Jack reappeared in the camp some time after, working for a neighbour, but took flight at a sudden alarm of Indians; and I am inclined to think his dread of them was the real cause of his leaving us so quickly. The ditch came to a stand-still for some time after he went, as we had so many other things to attend to.

We began making corrals for our horses and to contain our future sheep. Our land was extremely suitable for cattle, from the abundant supply of water always at hand, but we were advised not to keep any number at present, as they were so great an attraction to the Indians, who, as I before said, do not come for sheep, and were therefore unlikely to molest us if we had no cattle to tempt them.

The (or in English, the farmyard) were on one side of our ditch; on the other we began to enclose a small garden for vegetables; flowers we had no time to attend to at present.

After a few weeks our settlement began to look rather comfortable, and we thought a few milking cows would be a desirable addition. Lisada assured us we might get some at Saladillo, and he and I accordingly set off one day, intending to purchase a few. Saladillo was about fifteen miles off to the north-east of us, and consisted of about twenty mud huts, inhabited only by natives. There was a post-house in the place, where the diligence left our letters, and our first business was always an eager enquiry as to whether there were any for us.

While waiting outside the pulperia I saw in the distance three figures on horseback, in broad-brimmed straw hats, riding towards us down the long, hot, dusty road; and, as they came near, was delighted to see they consisted on the T.s, accompanied by their soldier servant, who had been with Charlie in his old regiment, and insisted on following his young master to the New World.

After a warm greeting I found they had just ridden from Rosario, and were en route for Cordoba, but intended to stay a few days at Monte Molino. As soon as Lisada and I had concluded our purchase, which consisted of four cows, for which we paid about 2l. each, we all rode back together.

We had been delayed some time by one thing and another, the T.s having to procure fresh horse, &c., and at last it became so late that Charlie and Gerald rode on, leaving Lisada and myself to drive the cows; and though these animals, like the sheep, get more rapidly over the ground in the River Plate than they do in England, we could not consider it desirable to urge milking cows out of a slow trot. After a little time we were left in complete darkness, and Lisada's horse became too tired to move a step farther. He was obliged, therefore, to unsaddle him, and leave both horse and saddle for the night, marking the place where he left the latter by burning a little grass round it. He then mounted behind me, and in this affectionate manner we got safely to our home, which could be seen for some miles across the dead flat of the country. Lisada, like all the natives, was very superstitious, and much afraid of darkness, and cheered me by various gloomy tales of horror as we rode along. As we passed a place called, from some unpleasant association or other, "Monte del Diablo", he said in a low voice, "Lugar de mal nombre" (that is, a place of the bad name), for, like the old Grecks or Romans, the natives consider it unlucky to allude more particularly to any subject of evil omen.

The T.s stayed with us some days and then went off to Cordoba, leaving their servant with us. Their arrival was a break in our monotonous life, and cheered us all up. G. had now become tolerably resigned to camp life, but certainly did not take to it warmly at first. He disliked the natives extremely, and on a first acquaintance they certainly are not fascinating to an Englishman, though often handsome, and with graceful, dignified manners, which appear to belong to them naturally. The lowest Gaucho has a wonderful advantage over the most respectable English labourer in manner and address, and will take of his hat and begin a conversation with you as politely as the most finished don, and use words and phrases such as no uneducated countryman of my own would dream of employing; but when one comes to essentials, I fear their moral and religious character is rather below that of an average ticket-of-leave man. It is very melancholy to come to such a conclusion about the people among whom one lives, but it seemed to me as if no kindness or confidence could excite any return of grateful feelings, and the utter want of morality is enough to call down a curse on any nation. The passing traveller who describes "The noble Gaucho", &c., does not easily see this; their courteous manners concealing their real character during a short acquaintance.

One's idea of how great a nation the Spaniards must have been is much raised by seeing how long their descendants have kept the impress of their refinement and self-controlled manners amid such different scenes; but the Church of Rome certainly appears to very little advantage in a country where she has long held such sovereign sway; and missionaries might indeed do a good work among these so-called Christians. I must own that we were not particularly fortunate in the specimens we came across, our household being rather like King David's army, to which "every man who was broken or had run away from his master joined himself" as we were supposed to be beyond the reach of all law or order, and our capataz Lisada - a handsome, clever man, to whom we at first took a great fancy - was celebrated at Frayle Muerto as being the very worst character in the whole country. He professed a great regard for us, but cheated us, I believe, on every possible occasion, and did no work he could possibly avoid. His redeeming point was his courage, and perhaps, in his own peculiar way, he may have had a liking for us. He was soon joined by his wife and two children, who were used to a wild neighbourhood, Lisada having on one occasion defended them successfully in a mud rancho from a sudden attack of Indians, with no better weapon than an old horse-pistol, the unfortunate woman concealing herself behind the door with her baby in her arms, holding her hand on its mouth lest its screams should betray her presence. We had some difficulty in holding communication with them at first, as the natives never learn any English; but we soon picked up enough Spanish for the purposes of ordinary life. It was now early in December, and we began to consider how we could properly celebrate Christmas; and, as I was obliged to go down to Buenos Ayres on business, I resolved to make some purchases in honour of the season. I ordered materials for a large plum pudding, and various other luxuries; but, unfortunately, none of them arrived till about the beginning of January, so we could only drink everyone's health in England in caña; and, as the thermometer stood at 90° in the shade (rather hot for the usual Christmas pleasures), we drove down in our cart to the river, and tried to amuse ourselves by fishing and talking over old Christmas meetings in Warwickshire, in days when we did not expect that fate would ever transplant us to such different scenes.

We now began to think seriously of purchasing sheep; and early in the new year I started with G. and Lisada on an expedition to Sauce, a small town on the frontier, in which was one of the forts intended to keep out the Indians. We had heard there were some sheep to be sold at a place close by, and, as Sauce was about sixty-six miles to the south of us, we started early in the morning, and reached the estancia late that night. We were hospitably received by the capataz and his wife, and found ourselves sufficiently improved in Spanish to converse with them on the state of the country. They told us an alarming story of the late possessor of the estancia Don Victorino and his headman having been killed, in a fight with the Indians just outside the house, about a year before, when he and the capataz, who stood bravely by his master, had made an attempt to rescue their cattle from these invaders. The estancia now belonged to his nephew, who, not unnaturally, preferred residing at Cordoba and leaving his capataz to manage the property. This was the first account of Indian attacks that we had seriously believed, and it made us rather grave; but we consoled ourselves by the thought that we were sixty miles farther from the frontier, and, therefore, not very likely to attract the notice of those marauders.

We found no sheep were to be had; so - after just riding into Sauce and visiting the pulperia, and further refreshing ourselves by a bathe, after which we rested under the willow grove from which the town is named (Sauce meaning willow) - we rode back to Monte Molino, starting just at sunset, and had a lovely ride by moon-light, reaching home about four in the morning

CHAPTER V

LOS INDIOS.

In the fairy tales that were my delight in earlier days, one member of a family after another used to start off in quest of anything that was much wanted by his relations, such as a purse always full of money, an enchanted sword, or some other equally useful article; and when one failed, another instantly went off on the same errand. The various expeditions that were made from Monte Molino in search of what was required, used often to remind me of these tales of my youth; at least, I am sure no hero of romance could have gone through more desolate regions than those we had to traverse on these occasions: the only difference was, that whereas, in the old stories, though the first two messengers always failed, the third met with equally invariable success, half-a-dozen of our ambassadors often went one after the other, without bringing back what was wanted, especially in later days, when something like the inexhaustible purse was wanted from Rosario, or something in the line of the enchanted sword, from our apathetic Government at Buenos Ayres.

As I had failed to procure any sheep at Sauce, Frank set forth in search of some we had heard of, at a still more distant spot, accompanied by M., a new acquaintance, who had only just arrived, but who soon bought a large tract of land close round Frayle Muerto, and is now one of the most enterprising settlers in the country.

Another young Englishman, S., had just purchased a piece of land only twelve miles from Monte Molino, and had now been there a few weeks. Others were heard of as likely to follow his example; and we hoped our country would soon be well peopled with English settlers.

We had engaged two new assistants to finish our ditch; an Irishman, also named Jack, a very good workman when sober, hilt with such a strong tendency to caña that we were obliged to withhold it him by force; and another helper he had brought with him, named Cabrero. We kept steadily at work after Frank left its, all trough March, and having completed the fortification round our house, began another ditch round a small quinta in which we intended to grow maize, &c. We also set to work to cut bricks, which hardened in the sun, and were then used to build outhouses for our servants to sleep in, and for other purposes.

Charlie T. had been down once, for a day or two, to leave all his newly-bought horses with us, and having completed his purchase of land at Cordoba, was gone away to Rosario to meet his brother; both intending shortly to join us, and begin building their house. Henry had left us some little time back, so our party at Monte Molino consisted now of G. and myself, and a cousin of Charlie T.'s, just come out form England, the T.s servant, and two Englishmen engaged to work for them: Jack, Cabrero, Lisada and his wife Salome, with her two little children, completed the household, making altogether twelve persons, of whom nine were full grown men.

Imagine us, then, about sunrise on a certain bright morning in April, just sitting down in the house to drink our coffee before beginning our work; the servants busy outside, and the faithful Lisada on the roof of the house, taking a bird's-eye view of the landscape, to see in what direction the horses had strayed in the night; driving them in for use during the day being always his first business. We now possessed about one hundred horses, the joint property of the T.s and ourselves; and on this particular morning they had strayed about two miles from the house to a fertile spot, where they were grazing with great satisfaction to themselves. We were quietly drinking our coffee and chatting together, when our peaceful meal was suddenly interrupted by a loud shout from Lisada, "Los Indios, caramba"* At this pleasing intelligence all three of us rushed hastily out, and beheld in the distance a body of horsemen advancing towards us at full gallop. The troop seemed to consist of two or three hundred, but we could not at first make out whether all the horses were mounted, as many appeared to us to have no riders, but Lisada and Cabrero declared that some of the Indians were clinging to the sides of their horses, according to their usual fashion when making an attack, so as to conceal their true numbers. At any rate, it was plain there was no time to be lost in preparing for our defence; so we ran the bullock-wagon into the gateway over the ditch, blocking up the passage, and snatched up our guns and pistols. I gave cach of the men a weapon as we had plenty of arms, took my own gun and revolver, and wait-

* *caramba* is a common expression of surprise, meaning literally - indeed!

ed for the attack. Poor Salome had rushed into the house with her two children and a small trunk, which I imagine contained all her valuables, and concealed herself in a dark corner, where, I afterwards found, she kept up spirits during these trying moments by smoking cigarettes.

In about ten minutes from the time of Lisada's shout of warning the Indians were within about four hundred yards of the house, and we then perceived that the actual number of men with whom we had to deal was about fifty, having with them a large troop of unmounted horses. These were now halted, and remained under the charge of three or four men who detached themselves from the main body, the remainder coming on at a hand-gallop until they had approached to within about fifty yards of the ditch, when they opened out their party, surrounding us on all sides, and again halted. I told my men not to fire until we were certain that their intentions were hostile; so we stood facing them, waiting until they should come close up. Lisada now shouted out that if they wished to fight we were quite ready to accommodate them, at which intimation a short parley took place among the Indians, after which three of them rode close up to the edge of the ditch, first leaving their long spears stuck in the ground, and one who was evidently a Gaucho, acting as interpreter, said that the cacique wished to speak with the owner of the estancia.

I therefore put down my gun and revolver, and walked forward to the edge of the ditch to meet the cacique and his two attendants, having first desired my companions to fire at once if they saw any symptoms of treachery. The conversation was conducted through the interpreter, as the two Indians could only speak a word or two of Spanish, and was begun by the cacique expressing a wish to come into our house, which polite offer I respectfully but firmly declined. He then told us he had lost his way, the party having come out on an expedition for hunting ostriches, and had not the least wish to injure us, but was, on the contrary, extremely anxious for our friendship.

While this conversation had been going on, the rest of the Indians had come up close behind the cacique, having also left their spears stuck in the ground; they talked rapidly among themselves, but of course we could not understand a word they said, and only two or three of them appeared to understand any Spanish. They were small wiry-looking men, with very black hair falling over their shoulders, flat faces with high cheek-bones, and no beard or whisker, and dark coppery complexions, with a repulsive expression of feature. All were dressed in the Gaucho costume as far as they were dressed at all, some few possessing decent clothes: one, I remember, wore an officer's coat, having probably murdered the unfortunate owner; but most of them were without hats, and had only a handkerchief tied over their matted locks, and all were excessively dirty.

The cacique, an old man with grey hair, was better got-up than the rest, wearing a large gaily-coloured poncho. Their arms consisted of spears about twenty feet long, many of them ornamented with bunches of feathers tied round the handles; and bolas, which they carried either round their waists or attached to the pommel of the saddle.

The conversation continued in the same amicable tone, the cacique next mentioning that he was very poor, and would be glad if we would give his men some clothes. This request I at once complied with, and brought out a few old things, presenting him with an old straw hat of my own, which he at once placed on his head with evident satisfaction. I also gave them some caña and tobacco, and Lisada and our other peon, seeing the friendly turn affairs had taken, crossed the ditch and handed cigarettes to our visitors, conversing with the interpreter, the only one of the party who dismounted. Whether this excellent man had been previously known to our equally respectable capataz, I cannot say, but they talked to each other with great apparent interest. The Gauchos who reside with the Indians have usually committed some atrocious crime which places them beyond the pale even of Gaucho civilisation.

The cacique made repeated declarations that nothing should induce him to injure his new and dear friends, or tempt him to touch their horses, and as we felt very uneasy lest they should fall in with Frank and his companions, whom we were every day expecting with the sheep, we said something about them, when the obliging cacique assured us again that, being friends of ours, they need fear nothing from him.

After staying nearly an hour they all rode slowly off, but before they went we crossed the ditch one by one, and shook hands with the cacique, who was able to say "Adios amigo". We were watching the departure of our unexpected and unwelcome visitors with feelings of extreme joy, when, to our dismay, we suddenly saw them all draw up on the rising ground about a mile from our house, when half their party rode towards our horses, and in a few minutes they had driven them up to their own troop of unmounted horses, and the whole body were off like the wind, in a northerly direction. It was impossible to pursue them, as we had only three indifferent horses, on one of which, however, Lisada galloped after them for some little distance, shouting like a madman, but I am sure he had not the least intention of overtaking them.

We could only gaze after our beloved steeds as they disappeared from our sight, and use expressions of a nature stronger than "caramba". Lisada. exhausted all his vocabulary, and for the matter of that so did we ours; but it was all in vain - horses and Indians had vanished like a dream.

After about an hour a few straggled back, and we eventually recovered about four or five. As the cacique had kindly promised to visit us again on his way back, we felt afraid his troop was only a small detachment, acting as scouts to a larger body of Indians; we therefore resolved to keep a strict look-out, and be ready to act on the defensive at a moment's warning. Lisada, who had seen the Indians before, assured us that it was only the sight of our arms that kept them from attacking us, and warned us not to believe a word they had said. We remained in a good deal of anxiety lest Frank and his party should fall in with them, and feared also, from the direction they had taken, they might next visit our new neighbour S., who was much less well provided with men and arms than we were; and this apprehension was much increased in the afternoon by the arrival of a native from Frayle Muerto, who told us he had seen a large body, of what he supposed to be Indians, going towards S.'s house, when he made off himself, with the greatest speed, to the "casa de fierro".

We saw no more, however, of the Indians that day, but in the afternoon we perceived something slowly crawling across the plain from the direction of Saladillo, which soon proved to be the T.s' bullock-carts, laden with their wooden house, furniture, &c.- in fact, all their property - which had luckily escaped the Indians, who had already appropriated all their horses.

A little latter in the day an Englishman, known as "Hairy Jim", arrived, in search of work; he, with the five men who had come with the bullock-carts, made a reinforcement of six to our garrison, and we now felt ready to defy any attack, as "Hairy Jim", so called from a long red beard, represented himself as "the bravest of the brave", and described thrilling adventures he had gone through with the Indians in the province of Buenos Ayres, were he said he had lived for many years. We invited this warlike character to remain with us for the present, and the T.s afterwards engaged him to work for them.

We kept watch in turns through the night, but had no fresh alarm. The next morning just as we were sitting down to breakfast, we saw five or six men galloping up, whom we of course took for Indians, and instantly sprang to our arms. But in a moment we saw that it was our neighbour S., with four companions, who had come down to see if we were still alive. S. then related his own interview with the Indians, and told us they had surprised him in the middle of the afternoon, just when he and two other companions were taking their siesta. A native woman, who acted as their cook, was lying asleep outside, under the shade of the cart, when she was most unpleasantly roused from her slumbers by seeing an Indian on horseback standing over her, telling her to get up behind him on his horse. She rushed in screaming to her master, and soon aroused the party, who came out with their arms, and instantly pulled up the board across their ditch.

The Indians then began to parley as they had done with us. S. told us that he had made up his mind that it was all over with him, as they were only three men to fifty Indians; and seeing the cacique had got on an old broad-brimmed hat which he recognised is mine, and also our horses, he naturally concluded we had all been murdered. He determined, however, to show that he was not afraid, thinking it his only chance, and told them they should not come into the house, but that he would give them some presents, on condition that they did not touch him or his horses, to which conditions the cacique again readily agreed. They became so friendly that S. begged him to change hats, wishing, he said, to keep a little remembrance of the supposed unfortunate owner; and this being done, the Indians departed, first playing the same trick as at Monte Molino, by driving off almost all his horses; but he was too much relieved at their departure to feel great grief at first, and as soon as he thought it safe to do so he rode down to see how we had fared.

After a good breakfast and a good talk over our adventures, we parted, and as no more was seen of the Indians we all soon returned to our usual way of life. Our anxiety about Frank was in a few days happily relieved by the arrival of M., who told us they had seen nothing of the Indians. They had purchased a large flock of sheep between them, which they had brought on safely to a place about ten leagues from us, called Los Perros, where there was a deserted house and corral.

M. had come to fetch G. and myself to assist in dividing the flock, half the sheep being M.'s property. We started off at once, taking a bullock-wagon for the weak lambs, and got to Los Perros the next evening, sleeping by the way at Los Algarobitas. I had to break to Frank the unwelcome intelligence of the loss of all our horses, which he bore with his usual philosophy, and we then set to work to part out the sheep. He had bought about two thousand, at about five shilling each, and they seemed a fine lot, in very good condition, especially considering they had travelled about a hundred miles. We got them safely up to Monte Molino in about a couple of days, and felt we were now really sheep-farmers.

CHAPTER VI

NEIGHBOURS - PROCEEDINGS OF THE DAY - LIONS - TIGERS - WOLVES - SNAKES - FROGS AND TOADS - BISCACHAS - VARIETY OF FOOD - ARMADILLOS - CARPINCHOS - IGUANAS - GREY FOXES - SKUNKS - WILD-FOWL

On our return from Los Perros we found that Charlie T. had arrived during our absence, bringing up with him a newly-found friend who was thinking of settling some-where in the country. He was a Southerner, a very nice fellow, and had been one of the officers of the Shenandoah. At the close of the war she was still cruising about, and only heard or its conclusion some months after peace had been proclaimed. Her crew were, of course, unable to return to their own country, and were now scattered in all directions. We all sympathised warmly with W., and pressed him to stay with us and settle close by, but, after some length of visit, he resolved to establish himself nearer to Rosario, and we often met there; but the last time I saw him he was preparing to return to the States, the Southerners having all received a free pardon.

Charlie was soon joined by his brother, and both set to work in good earnest to get their place, which they named Monte del Maiz, into order. We all helped them as much as we could. Our estancias were only three miles apart; and as their house - a wooden one, roofed with tiles, and promising to be very comfortable - took some months to put up, we all continued to live together.

We now made up a party of about fifteen, and had besides a good many occasional visitors; and, having no cook, took it by turns to act in that capacity, for which G. showed considerable abilities, preferring it to harder work. We neither saw nor heard anything more of the Indians for some months, and almost forgot their existence.

Our daily life was much like that in Entre Rios. We got up at sunrise, had a cup of coffee, and then went out to begin work. The peons had by this time driven in the horses, and our first occupation was to catch and saddle those wanted for the day. We next let out the sheep, who were always driven into the corral for the night; after this we busied ourselves about our garden, fencing, &c., as we were enclosing land for growing corn, alfalfa, and maize. Since the Indian invasion we had deepened and widened our ditch considerably, and had begun another, two hundred yards square, which surrounded our first enclosure of fifty yards, in which was the house.

We had been told that the Indians never drove off sheep, so we felt pretty secure about them. We had bought a few horses to replace our lost ones but it was long before our stud recovered the cruel ravages it had suffered. Our breakfast, à la fourchette, took place between eleven and twelve, then, after a couple of hours' rest in cool weather, and three or four hours' siesta in hot, we went to work again till sunset, when we dined; the rest of the evening we passed together, smoking, reading, chatting, until we felt inclined to retire to rest, which generally happened pretty early. This was the pleasantest period of our life in the Pampas; we were a cheerful party, all full of spirits, and thoroughly able to appreciate the feeling of extreme health and enjoyment, which the delightful climate and new fresh life give to all new comers. I can hardly imagine anything more exhilarating than a gallop in the fresh morning air over the free boundless plains; and when, in addition to this, one is riding over one's own land, everything about one being an object of interest, and with sanguine hopes of success to buoy one up, life seems very enjoyable. Such was our pleasant state just now, and, in spite of the disagreeable little episode of the Indians, we looked forward with confidence to making money rapidly.

We had now about three thousand sheep, which would be shorn in November, and would produce about twelve thousand pounds of wool, as the sheep here only yield about four pounds each; we had a great many lambs, and hoped our flock would increase as rapidly as Frank's had done in Entre Rios. We seldom left home at this time, and shooting was our chief amusement. There was great excitement one morning, on discovering that a lion had been among our sheep in the night, and had left about twenty dead. Their mode of attack seems to be to spring on the back of the sheep and then break its neck; at least, there was a mark under the throat, where the lion's claws had evidently grasped his victim, and then, apparently, had twisted round its head, until the unlucky sheep was strangled.

We instantly started in search of the enemy, and rode for some distance along the river-side before the dogs put him up out of the long grass. After a considerable chase we came up with him, and brought him to bay with two revolver balls through his body; the dogs then rushed in and took off his attention, while we dismounted from our horses, and Lisada gave him a coupe de gràce with an old rusty sword with which he had armed himself.

These lions, as they are called, are in reality pumas; they are rather like a tiger in shape, but are of a yellowish colour, and have no mane; the largest we ever killed measured nine feet from its nose to the end of its tail, and was considered by the natives to be a very large one: their ordinary length is about seven feet; this one was lassoed by Lisada and dragged till it was killed, which is the common native way of doing the business. Pumas do not willingly attack men unless brought to bay, but are very awkward customers when you come to close quarters with them. Two of our party hail a fight with one in the long grass, and, having fired away all their shots, wounding him severely, he made a spring at one of them, fortunately only scratching his arm and leg, his companion in the meantime beating the lion on the back of the head, until both it and the gun were flattened, and so despatching him. During the first year we killed about six; but they have now retired before settlers, and it is a rare thing to see them. They occupied a large space in the imagination of one of our party, who came in to me one day, declaring he had seen a lion which he at first took for a gateado (cat-coloured) horse, it was so large and had such a long-flowing mane; but on his nearer approach he discovered his mistake, as the supposed horse sat up and growled at him, and one of the dogs, going up to inspect it, received a blow from the lion's paw which made it run back howling; his horse, trembled violently under him and would not approach nearer, and the equally sagacious rider apparently sympathising with its feelings, both made the best of their way home; but no more was seen of the maned lion, the only one of the species I ever heard of here.

The jaguar, or South American tiger, abounds in parts of the country, especially in the large montes of Entre Rios and in the islands of the Parana, but we had very few round Frayle Muerto, and we never saw any, though a horse of ours, found dead one morning, was supposed, by the marks about it, to have been killed by a jaguar, as South American lions never attack horses. The jaguar skins are most beautifully marked, and worth from 3l. to 4l.; in Buenos Ayres some are even worth 8l.

We once also killed a wolf (yaguarras), but he must have strayed down accidentally from more wooded parts. There are numbers of them in the sierras of Cordoba; the skins are a beautiful reddish-brown, and they have very long hair.

These are the only animals that can be called dangerous, except the reptiles. There are great numbers of snakes, some of them very deadly. The most venomous kind is that of the Vivora de la Cruz, so called from the mark of a cross on its head; it is a lovely colour, with alternate stripes of black, red, and white. The natives say that its bite is certain death, and I believe it to be very dangerous, though happily I never knew anyone bitten by it. There are a great many varieties of snakes, the commonest being a black one, from four to five feet long, which I believe to be nearly harmless. I came across one once which seemed to me nearly six feet long, and as thick as a man's wrist, but perhaps it had just made a good meal. Hairy Jim brought in a terrific account one day of a black snake he had just seen, describing it as about thirty feet long, and as thick as his leg, but he was rather celebrated for his encounters with snakes and Indians.

The natives have a great dread of serpents, and always remonstrated with me on my foolhardiness in attacking and killing any that I saw. We turned them up constantly in ploughing, and often found them in our gardens - indeed, a visit to the melon bed was always rewarded by the sight of three or four, but I never found one in the house after it was finished, which was a great comfort. To make up for their absence, we had enormous quantities of toads and frogs indoors, it being quite impossible to keep them out. They got behind our boxes, and into every possible corner, and we were often obliged to have a clearing out, when about fifty would be found in our bed-room and sitting-room. I used sometimes, on these occasions, to relieve my feelings by spitting a dozen of them on a sword, and though I fear I may be thought very cruel, it was trying, if one got up for anything at night, to put one's bare foot on a large cold thing like a lump of jelly. One of our neighbours was one day drawing on his boots, when he found something impeded his progress, and after stamping for some time and finding it still very uncomfortable, he pulled it off to see what was the matter, and found that he had been squashing up a frog. I always carefully emptied my boots after this before putting them on.

If the wells are not covered they soon get full of frogs, who keep up a tremendous croaking at night, and we could hear a perfect chorus of them from the river on a summer evening, quite a mile off. The toads are as active as everything else, and I sometimes watched them, when we had moved into our brick house, run ten or twelve feet up the wall, and then fall down with a sort of squash.

There were but few scorpions about us, and though the natives consider their bite very bad, I can answer for its harmlessness, as I was one day bitten on the toe by one, and though rather unpleasant at the time, a little ammonia soon removed all bad results. We were less troubled by insects than in Entre Rios, but had a very fair shire of them. Our worst enemies in the garden were the biscachas, who, with their little companions the burrowing owls, are to be found in countless numbers all over the Pampas. We tried stopping up their holes, but the only effectual means of getting rid of them is smoking them out with sulphur, for which a machine has been invented. They are uninteresting animals, about the size of a large hare, and most destructive among green things. Their skins are worth but little, being like that of an inferior rabbit, with short grey hair. We often ate the young ones for a change, but they are rather dry food, though endurable to a hungry settler, in a pie, or made into curry. We partook of many new creatures at different times; when other food was scarce we often tried a little potro meat (i.e. horseflesh)- not at all a bad thing, as the English are now just beginning to discover. Donkey and mule are also very palatable, the former being considered by the natives a great luxury. The country abounds in small armadillos, of which there are four or five different species, the commonest being the peludos and mulitas. The peludo has hair sticking out between the scales of its shell, and is almost a foot in length; the mulita has a smooth shell, and is rather smaller. Both are extremely good to eat, though some fastidious people turn up their noses at them; they are rather like a sucking pig, and we cooked them in the native fashion as follows: after being opened and cleaned, a spit was thrust through them, and they were roasted in their shell over the embers; when sufficiently done, the shell was broken off, and a delicious morsel awaited the epicure; but they were better cold than hot, being rather rich.

There are several other species of armadillo, of which the matajo is the most curious. He rolls himself into a hard ball on the approach of an enemy, becoming quite impervious to a dog's tooth or the hoof of a horse, and looking more like a ball of dark brown wood than anything else, as his head and tail, covered with hard scales, fit exactly into each other. Whenever other game failed us we were sure of a good meal of armadillo, as we had only to ride out with the dogs for an hour or so, and were certain to catch half-a-dozen. Of course the abundance of these animals renders the camp very unsafe for riding over, as the ground in most places is quite honeycombed with their holes, and you are almost sure to get a fall when galloping for any distance; but the camp is soft, and one is scarcely ever hurt. Of course the holes made by the biscachas are much larger, but they are not dangerous to anyone at all acquainted with the country, as you can always see, by the bareness of the ground round a biscachero, what to avoid; but the armadillos live in the long grass and it is quite impossible, when riding fast, to see their holes.

Another very common animal in some parts is the carpincho, or river pig, who lives in the river, and is rather like a common pig in appearance, only brown, and with longer hair. The natives eat him, but we never did, chiefly because we scarcely had any in our river. The skins are useful for saddles and belts. They are very shy animals, and difficult to kill.

The large lizard, or iguana, abounds, and is rather a ferocious-looking creature, about five feet in length, armed with long teeth, but is quite harmless, I believe, unless attacked. We had an absurd fight one day with an iguana, which we came across when out riding. Having wounded it with our revolvers, one of our party got down to finish it with hip whip, upon which it ran snapping at him, much to his consternation and our amusement, as they stood representing a sort of burlesque of St. George and the dragon; a fierce combat ensued, but our valiant champion was at length victorious, and slew the monster reptile. They will charge at anyone who attacks them, and can inflict a sharp blow on a dog with their tail, and rather a serious bite with their long teeth. We were never quite reduced to eating them, but they are said to be very good.

I forgot, in describing the beasts of prey, to mention great numbers of grey foxes, who were terrible enemies to our young lambs. We overcame our British prejudices, and killed them down a good deal. Their skins are very useful. The skunks were a great nuisance to us, as they would come at night and take our hens off their nests. Their presence was easily discovered, as anything more horrible than the odour they diffuse can hardly be imagined. I am sorry to say we have still many about, though we have shot at them whenever we could see as well as smell them. They are unfortunately not in the least timid, and would never run away, appearing aware of the advantage they had over us. I could truly say "their tameness was shocking to me", and they were a dreadful pest. Their ways and habits are really too unpleasant to describe further, though they are rather pretty little animals to look at - black and white, with soft hair and very bushy tails. I skinned one once, but it was too dreadful an operation to repeat. A visitor once captured one, which he skinned, under the impression that it was a new kind of squirrel, and brought it to me in triumph, saying, however, that he thought it a pity our squirrels had such unpleasant habits.

Our river, as I said before, abounded in every sort of wild-fowl, and whenever we had a little leisure we went down to shoot; towards evening was the best time, as then the ducks were flying in countless numbers towards their roosting-places. There are also quantities off wild swans and geese, and at one time of the year the lovely flamingoes came in flocks. To see them rising slowly in the air, the sun shining on their wings with every variety of shade, from the palest rose colour to the brightest scarlet, was a most beautiful sight. Our English relations were always exhorting us to send them some of these gaily-coloured feathers, which English ladies wear in their hats, on the same principle, I suppose, that the Indians ornament their spears with them; but I am afraid it was some time before I attended to these requests, having a good deal besides to do.

The river also abounded in nutrias, a kind of otter, the fur of which was in great request in the time of beaver hats, and is still of some value for rugs.

CHAPTER VII

A VISITOR FROM ENGLAND; THINKS OUR POSITION DANGEROUS - FRIGHTFUL TRAGEDY IN OUR NEIGHBOURHOOD.

Another new neighbour, T., had lately settled within about ten miles of us, on the Saladillo side. He was an officer in the English navy, and had been attracted away from it by the brilliant prospects supposed to be opening in the River Plate. He was soon joined by two brothers, John and James W., who had come across the Andes from New Zealand with a party of three others, and arrived during June. They were now busy digging their ditch and building a house, assisted by our truant Jack, who had suddenly reappeared. Their estancia was named Monte de la Lèña, and we could just see it from the top of our house as a dim speck in the distance. All three were very nice fellows, and a welcome addition to our little colony... Many other settlers were buying land near to Frayle Muerto, and we began to entertain sanguine expectations that our part of the country would soon be as populous as Entre Rios.

In August we had a visit from the T.s' father, who stayed a few days at our estancia, and then went on with his sons to Monte del Maiz, the house there being nearly completed. He had come out to have a look at the country and see his sons, and did not much approve of their proximity to the Indians.

There was now a good opportunity of buying land cheaply in Santa Fe, and Mr. T. having determined to buy an estate there for his sons, endeavoured to induce us to do the same, thinking that, notwithstanding the money we had laid out, it would be better for us all to move for a time to a more settled place, and return to our present abode when the position should be better defended. He pressed upon us that the Paraguayan war at present took of all the troops, and left the Indian invasions quite unchecked; this could not last for over, but meantime we might suffer severely. We none of us liked the idea of moving, but the T.s at length decided, after much deliberation, to do so for a time. We, however, came to the conclusion that we should do better to remain where we were, and take our chance; whether we judged wisely or not only time can show. There certainly came a period at which we regretted that we had not followed Mr. T.'s kind advice.

We were all much cast down at the prospect of parting with such good neighbours and friends, as we could not expect to meet very often when one hundred miles apart; they did not, however, finally move away for some months. All this time things seemed to be going on in a very promising way, and we were looking forward with much pleasure to a visit, which my eldest brother and an old college friend had written to say they intended to pay us during the autumn holidays; we calculated they would arrive early in October. Mr. T. did not stay beyond August; and everything went on much as usual until the end of September, when an event happened which cast a most dreadful gloom over our little colony.

Among the new settlers in the neighbourhood were two young Englishmen who had just come to a place about fifteen miles from us, called Monte Llovedor, where they had already put up a small fort surrounded by a ditch, and were shortly going to build a house. Some of our party had ridden over to see them one day, and found one of the partners, P., was away on business; the other, Edwardes, was hard at work, assisted by his headman, Dan Mulligan, two Englishmen who had at one time worked for us, and two peons. We left about the middle of the afternoon, the Irish capataz or headman, Dan Mulligan, accompanying us, to bring back a horse which Edwardes had purchased from us, intending to sleep at our house, and return with it the next day. The first intelligence, however, that greeted us next morning, was a report brought in by our peons that the Indians were again about; and the capataz accordingly delayed his return for a couple of days, fearing that he should fall in with them. Nothing more having been seen or heard of any invaders, he started in the afternoon with the horse, and the following morning G. and Lisada rode out to see whether they could obtain any news, intending also, if the Indians really had been in the neighbourhood, to pick up any stray cattle they might have left behind them.

They rode for about nine miles without seeing anything, but then suddenly came upon traces of a large Indian encampment close to the river, where a number of things of no value, evidently the property of English settlers, were lying strewed about on the ground. Among them was a book which they picked up, and at once returned with it, and when it was dry we with some difficulty made out P.'s name written in the first page.

This discovery alarmed us much for the safety of our new neighbours, but it was too late to do anything that afternoon, and we were forced to wait till the next morning, when Frank, Lisada, and myself started off, well armed and mounted on our fastest horses, to see whether anything was amiss at Monte Llovedor. We kept a good look-out for Indians during our fifteen miles' ride, but saw nothing to alarm us till we got near the place, when the first glance showed us that the fort was entirely destroyed, and instead of the cheery welcome that had greeted our arrival five days ago, we were only received by a mournful howling from all the dogs. We rode close up to the ditch, where a dreadful scene of devastation met our eyes. The fort was in ruins, all burnt and blackened, and over it were the charred remains of the two carts; the bullock trunks stood near, broken open, and all the contents which the Indians had not cared to take away, such as letters, books, &c., lay strewed about in every direction.

We dismounted, and having tied up our horses, began to make further investigations into the fate of our unfortunate neighbours, and finding nothing at first, were beginning to hope they might have escaped, when we suddenly perceived in the ditch three bodies, two lying close to the little fort, and one by the drawbridge in the outer ditch. They were loosely covered with earth, which led us at first to hope they were Indians, as they were so much blackened that it was difficult to make out what nation they belonged to. They were, however, in reality, the bodies of poor Edwardes and his two English workmen, though we only discovered this a little later. We were pursuing our mournful search, when happening suddenly to raise our eyes, we saw in the distance a number of horse-men approaching from several sides. Thinking, of course, that the Indians were returning, we instantly ran into the little fort, and prepared to defend ourselves as best we could.

The party seemed in no great hurry to reach us, and two of their number rode slowly forward as if reconnoitring. They at length came near for us to see them clearly, when we perceived, to our great joy, that they were natives, and not Indians. They seemed equally relieved at making a similar discovery about us, and the whole body then rode up, when we found them to consist of a sort of scratch troop hastily got together, headed by Don Nasario Casas, the Comandante of Frayle Muerto.

They were supposed to be in search of the Indians, but they had taken very good care not to come out until the enemy had all made off. They presented a most curious appearance, armed in a miscellaneous way, with any old weapon they could lay their hands on, old swords, lances, &c., and each man was most carefully leading his best horse, on which he evidently intended to escape in case the enemy should come in sight. From them we learned that the Irish capataz, after leaving us, had ridden straight back to Monte Llovedor, which he reached just at sunset; but the moment he arrived he perceived the fearful catastrophe that had taken place, and, having got a glimpse of the dead bodies, was just about to dismount from his horse to examine them, when he saw in the distance twelve or fourteen men galloping towards him at full speed. It was rapidly becoming dark, so he made off as quickly as possible to S.'s estancia, which was about ten miles off. Darkness favoured him, and having a good start of the Indians, after galloping some miles he got away from his pursuers, and at last seeing no more of them, and being unable to go farther in the complete darkness, he resolved to unsaddle his horse and wait for daylight. He lay down, and in spite of his dangerous position fell asleep for a few hours, but just as it became light found he was near S.'s estancia, to which he at once rode up and told them what had happened. S. got together all the Englishmen he could from the neighbouring estancias, and they rode down to examine the spot, when they recognised the bodies as those of poor Edwardes and his two English workmen, and covered them lightly with earth until they could be taken away and properly buried. This had been done the day before our visit, and S. and his party then went on into Frayle Muerto to give notice to the Comandante of what had occurred.

Don Nasario had himself lost about one thousand five hundred head of cattle, and was now come out, he said, to endeavour, after examining the spot, to overtake the Indians, and get back some of his property. We all remained at the fort some time longer, and I had a narrow escape myself from an old rusty fowling-piece going off close to my head in the hands of one of these unskilful militia; upon which Don Nasario assured him that instant death would have been his fate had I been in the least injured.

Nothing more could be done, and we at last separated and rode slowly home, having first agreed that the bodies of our unfortunate countrymen should be shortly taken down to Rosario and properly buried, which was soon after done. It was strange by how mere a chance, apparently, two of the usual inhabitants of the estancia escaped, sharing the fate of the others; P., the other owner, who was returning home, having stopped at the Algarobitas, which was the nearest estancia, for the night, intending to return early the next day; and the Irish capataz having, in consequence of our visit, returned with us, only two or three days before the Indians came; indeed, we all narrowly escaped falling in with them.

When the first panic had subsided, all the settlers endeavoured to learn the exact particulars of this sad affair; but we had only the account of the native peon, whom at first we strongly suspected of treachery. I now think, however, that our suspicious were erroneous; the boy had been carried off by the Indians, and was never seen again.

The account which the peon gave was as follows:

Very soon after dark, on the evening of the day on which our party had visited Monte Llovedor, all the men were busy preparing supper in their tent, when they suddenly heard a rush of horsemen, and, guessing at once what it was, seized their arms and ran into the fort, which they had only that day completed. The Indians, who were supposed to be about two hundred in number, surrounded the whole place, and told them that, if they would come out and give up everything they had, their lives should be spared. The sides of the fort were built of sods of earth and thatched with grass, thickly covered with mud, supposed to be able to resist fire. There was a deep outer ditch round the whole enclosure, which was about fifty yards square, in the middle of which the tent was pitched, the fort being in one corner, with a second ditch round it; but poor Edwardes and his partner had committed the unlucky mistake of leaving the earth thrown out of the ditch in a heap round it, which, of course, formed a shelter for the enemy to creep up behind. There was a small drawbridge across the ditch, which the besieged party pulled up; and, seeing what a strong force the Indians had, Edwardes told them they might take any thing in the tent, but that, if they attempted to enter the fort, he should fire on them.

While he was talking, the treacherous Indians surrounded him, getting into the ditch, where they began poking the sides of the fort with their long lances; upon which the Englishmen fired upon them, but it was so dark they could not see whether they hit any of their assailants. The Indians then collected bunches of dried grass, which they lighted and pushed under the caves with their lances, soon setting fire in this way to the roof. After a short time the smoke and heat became so unbearable that the three all rushed out together, and were instantly murdered by the Indians. The native slipped into the ditch with the boy in front of him, first instructing the latter to say he was quite young, and to implore them to spare his life. The boy and native were immediately pulled out by the Indians, who were about to despatch the man, when some Gauchos who were with them pleaded for his life, and, as he was already wounded in the leg, they contented themselves with stripping him. He recognised one of the Gauchos, who interceded for him, as having been up to the fort a short time before, with a horse they had bought, when he was probably acting as an Indian spy. This man advised him to make the best of his way off, as, if he fell in with any stray Indians, they would be sure to kill him. He reached an English estancia next morning where he told his story, and was taken into Frayle Muerto to the doctor, his leg being very badly wounded. He always stuck to this account, when questioned by anyone; so we at last concluded it must be true; and there could, of course, be no doubt that our poor neighbours had been murdered by the Indians.

The natives declared that they found some Indian graves to the south freshly made, so we all hoped some of the shots had taken effect. P. soon after abandoned a spot so full of melancholy recollections, and settled in Rosario; but it was long before the painful impression caused by this event passed away from the neighbourhood; and it had a most disastrous effect, in quite checking, for a time, the numerous emigrants, who were beginning to settle round us.

CHAPTER VIII

FRAYLE MUERTO - THE FONDA - INCREASE OF THE TOWN - ITS OFFICIALS - HEALTHINESS OF THE CLIMATE.

Letters from England made us now expect that my brother and his companion might shortly arrive, as it was now the beginning of October, and, from calculating the probable time taken up by the voyage, we felt they must already have reached Buenos Ayres; a few days, therefore, after the sad event recorded in my last chapter, I started for Frayle Muerto, taking horses with me for them to ride out, and there I for some days awaited their arrival. Frayle Muerto had advanced many steps in civilisation since our arrival at the post-house fifteen months before. The railway from Rosario was now open as far as this point, and the temporary station had something of the appearance of a similar one in some country place at home; the foundations of a grand permanent station were laid, and when finished, a few months later, it was quite as good, and arranged much in the same way, as in any ordinary town in England. Indeed, strange as it may seem, the railway waiting-room always gave me a much more homelike feeling than anything else in the country; and I use to look quite affectionately at the clerk, dispensing the tickets through the square pigeonhole, and all the other little things that reminded me of old England.

The traffic on the line increased daily, as even the natives, slow as they are to adopt any improvements, began to discover that their goods accomplished the one hundred and thirty miles between Rosario and Frayle Muerto much more rapidly by rail than in the tortoise-like bullock-carts; and there was a great deal of passenger traffic, the English settlers finding it now much more frequently necessary to go down to Rosario on business than when the journey entailed two days' confinement inside the stuffy diligence. Besides the railway station there was a fonda, or small inn, a great improvement on the old post-house, kept by an Italian, named Don Pepe, supposed to be a count in his own country.-I believe he was a man of good family, obliged to leave Italy for some political reasons. He was very popular with the English settlers, being always ready to oblige and help them in every way; but he maintained a stern and imposing demeanour towards the natives, whom he detested, declaring them to be 'muy picaros', and possessing various other amiable qualities.

The fonda contained three rooms, one of which was used for the bar, and served also as a sort of general shop, which supplied heterogeneous articles of every description. The next apartment was the dininig-room, turned at night into a bed-room; when the mingled odour of garlic, oil, caña, and tobacco smoke rendered the air not of the most balmy description. Never in my life did I enter this apartment without finding one or two inmates who had evidently had a great deal more caña than was good for them, and generally, I am sorry to say, the number of these unpleasant companions was much larger. The other room was a sleeping-room, reserved for the superior guests, including, of course, all the English settlers. Don Pepe never allowed the Gauchos to penetrate beyond the bar, but, even with all he could do, the fonda was a rough place, unsuited to the fastidious; still, it was very superior to anything ever known before, and looked upon by the weary travellers, fresh from roughing it in the camp, as a sort of haven of delight.

Don Pepe was assisted in his labours by a partner, Luigi by name, generally supposed to have been a brigand and indeed he had no objection to admit as much, stating that he had been previously brought up as a priest, but had left his ecclesiastical studies for a more stirring life. He used worse language than anyone I ever met with, but was so much alarmed during the cholera time, two years ago, by a sharp attack which nearly brought him to the grave, that for some time afterwards his conversation would have been fit for the ears of his early associates, some of his old ideas having, I suppose, returned to his mind. He was a good-tempered fellow, and much liked in spite of his faults, both by Don Pepe and his English guests.

An Englishman started another fonda, which went on for some time, during which we all thought it our duty to patronise him; but want of capital soon forcing him to retire from the contest, Don Pepe now has it all his own way, and also manages the refreshment-room at the station, the first contractor, a Hungarian Jew, having moved on to Villa Nueva.

It is curious how cosmopolitan one gets living in any part of the New World; and no one who has only seen the other side of the Atlantic can, I think, entirely understand the state of society in the two Americas. Some of one's British prejudices are removed and some strengthened; one feels confirmed in the first article of a Briton's creed, that there is no place like England, and no people like Englishmen, but one feels also that other nations possess kind feelings and warmth of heart; and circumstances arise occasionally, showing that "one touch of nature makes the whole world kin". This, I must add, does not include the Indians.

But to return to Frayle Muerto. A good many new houses had been built in the town, which now contained about a thousand inhabitants. The leading characters in the place were, first, Don Cleto del Campillo, who was, in fact, the only real gentleman there. He was descended from one of the best old Spanish families in the River Plate, and his father had held a high office under Government, both in America and Europe. Don Cleto was a very well educated and agreeable man, with a great admiration for Shakespeare - a good test of a foreigner's literary taste in the eyes of a Briton. He was always most pleasant and kind to the English, whom, he says, he considers one of the first nations in the world, having a great contempt for the Gauchos. Don Cleto had originally been a rich man, and at this time still possessed a good deal of property, both near Frayle Muerto and round Cordoba. Our friend and neighbour M., whom I previously mentioned, has, however, bought most of his property round Frayle Muerto, and I fear Don Cleto may intend to remove to Cordoba.

Don Nasario was the next in rank. He commanded a fluctuating band of soldiers, which generally appeared to me to amount to about twelve in number. This efficient troop, and any volunteers who could be got together on the spur of the moment, at this time constituted the whole national defence against Indian invasions.

The police arrangements were conducted by the "Juez de Paz", a dignitary who held office for a year, and was elected by votes in the district. This important post was last held by a leading shoemaker, Don Benigno. The operations of justice were conducted in the house of the person in temporary authority, and were generally pretty summary.

I could never quite discover who or what the police were, but when anyone was to be taken up, an individual in no particular dress, armed with a drawn sword, would appear, and march the victim off to prison. The 'cuartel' was a small room close to the guard-house, so that the military force could be called in whenever the civil proved inefficient. The Comandante possessed the power of life and death, and excentions were not uncommon.

A man working for us at one time was put to death under the following circumstances.

He had deserted from the army, having murdered one of his officers, and came to us in search of work, which we gave him, not, of course, being aware of his previous conduct; but after working for us a short time he took it into his head to go into the town, for some purpose or other, and being there recognised by an officer who had known of his crime, and happened to be passing through Frayle Muerto, he was instantly arrested, tried, and shot.

He quite brought his death upon himself, having, previously been warned by the judge to leave the town, and told that while he continued quietly working out in the camp he should be unnoticed, but if he persisted in remaining in the town, drinking and gambling, he would be taken up for trial. He remained in spite of the warning till recognised by the officer, whose demand for his punishment could not be disregarded, and he certainly deserved his fate.

The priest was an Italian, and not a very clerical character, but pleasant and good-natured, and having been educated as a doctor, did all he could for the bodies of his parishioners, and I trust also for their souls. What curious vicissitudes of life had at length landed him in this secluded part of the Argentine Republic I do not know, but he was a well-informed man, acquainted with several modern languages, and a very pleasant companion. He came into the fonda at one time for his meals, while his house was building, and it was there I used to see him. During the cholera time he exerted himself nobly for the people, and I hope may have made some lasting impression on them.

The Gauchos make a perfect jest of everything connected with religion, and are scarcely ever seen inside a church, appearing to think that the women can do all that is necessary for them. The church was of brick, a small, ugly building, with a single bell hung up outside; the altar adorned in the usual tawdry fashion. There are schools in all towns of this size, I believe, under the control of Government, and reading and writing are taught in them, but very little religious instruction, if any, given. All townspeople can read and write, but these are very uncommon accomplishments out in the camp, and a Gaucho who possesses both always takes care to let you know his powers, of which he is not a little proud. The women, as a rule, are better educated than the men, and can mostly read and write, though Salome was an exception, and sometimes requested me to read her letters to her. The correspondence was not highly interesting.

The only person who remains to be described is the doctor. He was a clever little man, well informed about, general things, and devoted to gardening. He was very kind in giving us seeds and vegetables for our newly-made beds, and always welcomed us hospitably at his house, where his pretty niece, Doña Flores, did the honours in a very attractive way, and made it rather an agreeable resort.

As to Don Bartolo's medical skill, I never tested it but once, when I did not find it very efficacious; but I am bound to add I was suffering from rheumatism, which is a difficult complaint to cure in all countries.

We usually acted as our own doctors, as it was not very convenient to send thirty miles for a physician; indeed we might have sent a good many times before any body would have come, Monte Molino being regarded in Frayle Muerto much as an expedition to the Highlands was regarded by Baillie Nicol Jarvie in .'Rob Roy'; and, besides this, the poor doctor was so lame from two club feet, an ailment quite beyond the skill of Argentine surgeons to cure, that he was hardly able to limp about the town. I was therefore obliged to turn medico on my own account, and was rather proud of my success on one occasion in setting a broken thigh. One of our boys, Venero, had just captured a sheep he had been ordered to bring up, and was riding towards the house with it in his arms, when his horse ran away with him, and fell over the wire fencing, where a universal smash of horse, boy, and sheep having taken place, the natives ran in to inform me that Venero was 'quebrado' (broken). I went out, hardly knowing what to expect, and soon discovered that he had fractured his thigh, and as it was, of course, necessary to send him to the doctor, I thought he would suffer less from thirty miles bumping over the camp in a bullock cart, if his leg was first set even in my unprofessional way. I therefore made some small wooden splints, and having put his leg in the proper position, I bound it firmly up with strips of linen, in spite of piteous outcries from my patient. He was then despatched to the doctor, who pronounced the limb properly set, and merely tightened the bandages a little; in about six weeks Venero returned, as well able to use his legs as ever, and I used to look at him with considerable pride.

The natives came constantly to me for 'remedios', which they always swallowed with the most undoubting faith. The healthy life they lead renders their constitutions wonderfully good, and they recover from any accident or illness in a most rapid way. The climate is certainly very healthy, and the Gauchos never suffer from fever or ague, which do not readily attack foreigners; though, of course, it is possible to have fever, as I myself experienced. In general all new comers to the country enjoy remarkably good health. The only peculiarity which I am quite unable to account for is, that in spite of the large amount of fresh pure air, they find any cuts or wounds very difficult to cure; and lockjaw will come on from the most trifling accident. A poor friend of my own died of it, brought on by what appeared to be merely a slight scratch in his little finger, on which he unhappily put sticking-plaster; lint and cold water being the proper remedies. He was in Buenos Ayres at the time, and, of course, within reach of good doctors, but they were quite unable to save him.

Any little cut takes a long time to heal, and generally leaves a scar; but we always found cold water dressings, applied at once, a safe remedy.

The natives must have suffered terribly within the last few years from smallpox, as in some parts of the country three persons out of every five are marked with it; but, whenever it came, I suppose it exhausted itself, as I never heard of any case. The only general epidemic I myself witnessed was the dreadful visitation of cholera a little later, which I shall describe by and by.

CHAPTER IX

FURTHER ARRIVALS - LOAFERS - SHEEP DRIVING - OUR DOGS.

I remained some days in Frayle Muerto in hopes of hearing some news of the arrival of my brother and his friend, residing, of course, at Don Pepe's splendid establishment. Some of the English settlers were constantly in and out of the town, and our colony could now boast of some ladies, who had recently arrived. Mr. F. and his wife had recently established themselves at an estancia, about four leagues from the town, where they were building a house; and, one league out of the town, a place called 'Las Chañaritos' had just been taken by a numerous family, lately arrived in the colony. They consisted of five brothers, one of whom had a wife and two or three little children, and two sisters; these ladies all being very pleasant and lively, Las Chañaritos became a popular resort. They belonged to an old family in the county Clare, and possessing the spirit in which the Irish are never deficient, bore the various hardships and difficulties inseparable from first settling, with the greatest cheerfulness, and appeared quite indifferent to the Indians, from whom, of course, their near neighbourhood to the town made them much safer than if they had been farther out in the camp, though there was really nothing beyond Don Nasario and his twelve soldiers to prevent their coming into Frayle Muerto and carrying off anything they might take a fancy to.

After waiting vainly for some days without any tidings of my friends' arrival, I was forced to return to Monte Molino, trusting they would find their way out to us, whenever they might arrive. I kept a good look out for Indians during my ride home, but saw no signs of them, and found on my return that there had been no fresh alarm, though we supposed them to be still hovering about the camps.

The weather became terribly wet and stormy, and for a few days we neither saw nor heard anything of our expected guests.

I was sitting rather gloomily in the house one afternoon, a severe 'temporal' raging outside, having just abandoned all hopes of finding, any spot where drops of water should not descend slowly on my head, like the drippings from a leaky shower-bath before the victim takes courage to pull the string, and was endeavouring to forget my trials in the settler's unfailing solace, a pipe, when I suddenly descried two drenched horsemen galloping up to the house, and was delighted to perceive that one of them was my brother, making his way across the camp under the guidance of a peon.

After a joyful meeting we proceeded to make him as comfortable as circumstances would permit. He, of course, arrived in a very hungry state, not inclined to take a much more cheerful view of the Argentine Republic than poor G. had done on his first arrival. I found that he and his friend Hume had come up by train from Rosario, and reached Frayle Muerto on the afternoon of the very day I had left it; having fallen in with our neighbour T. in the train, they had been hospitably pressed by him to come on to Monte de la Lèña, as the easiest way of caching us. They accordingly rode out, intending to sleep there, and come on next day, but found all at the estancia in momentary expectation of an attack from Indians; under these circumstances their kind host would not hear of their running the risk of riding across the camp, but insisted on their remaining till all fear of the Indians was over. They waited three days, during all which time a storm was raging incessantly, and the house being nothing but a mud rancho, put up for temporary use, streams of water poured in on every side. They were all shut tip in one room, the furniture of which was limited to three or four wooden stools and a table, and there were few resources for amusement, beyond the constant expectation of an attack from the Indians. The meals were served up in a tin pan and pannikin, and there was a great scarcity of provisions, the party on the last day being all reduced to live on raisins. This was rather a change for two travellers fresh from the London season, and my brother being unable to bear it any longer resolved at last to take his chance of the Indians, and T. refusing to allow him to walk over, as he proposed, furnished him with a horse and guide, with which he started.

I went over the next day to welcome Hume to the new country, and found him very much disgusted indeed with everything, excepting T.'s kind hospitality. The sun began to shine, however, as we rode back to Monte Molino, talking over old college days and present things at the same moment; I making inquiries for friends at home, and Hume uttering remarks more forcible than flattering, as to the country, natives, and general state of things, amid which he suddenly found himself in the Frayle Muerto camps.

As we rode up to the house we descried Walter, already armed with a spade, at work in the garden, and projecting all sorts of improvements, having quite forgotten the unpleasant three days at Monte de la Lèña; and Hume having been brought to the same cheerful way of viewing things, by some rest and food, we held a long discussion with these new advisers, as to whether we should follow Mr. T.'s advice and remove to Santa Fe, or remain on here and trust to keeping off the Indians until peace with Paraguay enabled the Government to defend the frontiers properly. The general vote was for remaining and our new councillors agreed with us that we ought as soon as possible to begin building a larger house, hinting that the present abode was hardly a sufficient residence for five inmates, usually favoured with half a dozen guests.

Hume told me that, in spite of his feelings of disgust on reaching Monte de la Lèña, his opinion of the country had so far improved as to make him wish to try a few years of it, and that, if we were willing to take him, he would join us as a third partner. We readily agreed to this, as an increase of numbers was very desirable in the disturbed state of the country, and, of course, an old friend was a welcome addition to our party. This being arranged, he wished, before settling down, to see a little of the country; and, my brother being anxious to make the most of his time, they both set off for Santa Fe. They went by train as far as Tortugas, a railway station about half way between Frayle Muerto and Rosario, and, having there procured some horses, started off across the camp, intending to pay a visit to K. and his party at Las Rosas, the estancia which I mentioned in a former chapter.

As might have been naturally expected, they very speedily lost their way, the flat green plains being extremely confusing to new comers, as the slight indications which are enough to guide an old inhabitant in the camp are almost imperceptible at first; and my brother said it reminded him forcibly of being at sea on dry land. They were reduced to sleeping out, and soon found themselves a prey to most savage attacks from the inexorable mosquitoes, so much so that, by next morning, Hume declared to me that his nearest and dearest relations would not have known him. They were relieved to find that in the darkness they had been wandering about close to the estancia they were in search of, which they reached about breakfast time, receiving a kind welcome when they mentioned our names.

They were, however, at once introduced to a very wholesome custom which prevailed at Las Rosas, namely, that all visitors not provided with estancias of their own should make themselves useful, and at once join in whatever work was going on. Hume told me he was a little startled at finding himself expected to begin ramming posts in for wire fencing, immediately after finishing his breakfast, and while still almost unable to see from the effects of the mosquitoes; but a very short residence in the country made him approve most highly of the rules at Las Rosas.

And, having said this much, I cannot help slightly mentioning a habit much too prevalent among some men who come out to the country; namely, the taking an unfair advantage of the hospitality most readily shown by all settlers, and remaining for months, living at the expense of their hosts, without offering to assist in the work going on in any way. Such people ought to remember that all settlers recently arrived, having come out to make their fortunes, cannot possibly be rich; and it is extremely hard upon them to have a number of young men living upon them for weeks, and perhaps months, doing nothing whatever to assist in the work. I cannot myself understand how anyone can possibly feel comfortable under such circumstances. All the English settlers in Santa Fe and Cordoba had a strong feeling on this subject; and, though nobody over expected any work from a brother settler with a place of his own, who might come for a visit, we should none of us have thought of sitting with our hands before us, while our hosts were toiling hard for their livelihood. We all suffered a good deal from what we called the army of loafers, i.e. a number of young men come out from England, under pretence of becoming sheep-farmers, who simply passed their time in going from one estancia to another, merely amusing themselves, and staying as long as their entertainers would keep them; circulating, as I might say, through the country, till found by their hosts to be such completely worthless coin that they refused to pass them any more. Our very great distance from civilisation caused us at first to be less favoured with these sorts of guests; but, Las Rosas being only twenty leagues from Rosario, if the four partners had not made most stringent rules on the subject, and enforced them in a way that their previous experience of military discipline made easy, they would shortly, to use a common expression, have been eaten out of house and home by casual visitors. To real friends Las Rosas was the most hospitable of houses, and considered by us all as the model of an estancia. We were obliged, later, to adopt their rule about visitors working, as Frayle Muerto became better known, and the camps round us a great resort for new comers. The four proprietors of Las Rosas had put up a very fair house and good out-buildings, and had also enclosed a great deal of land. They had some hundred head of cattle, and a few sheep, but were turning their attention chiefly to agriculture; they lived very comfortably, and the estancia bid fair, in time, to be one of the most prosperous in Santa Fe; they were considered to be quite out of Indian range, and it was only about seven leagues from Las Rosas that the T.s intended to start their new place.

After about a fortnight's visit, Hume returned to us, my brother going on to Rosario, and intending to be a little longer absent, as he wished to see rather more of the country. Hume resolved to buy some sheep as soon as possible, and our neighbour M. having just brought up several thousand from Rio Cuarto, some of which he intended to dispose of, it seemed a very good opportunity for adding to our flock. The weather had become very sultry, and Hume suddenly reappeared after two or three days' absence, looking very hot and uncomfortable. He told us he had bought about eight hundred sheep, which he had driven along, by dint of superhuman exertions, to about four leagues from our estancia, until about the middle of the day, when they suddenly refused to move a step further, and all laid themselves down in the road, huddled up close together, such being the universal custom of Argentine sheep in hot weather, who, like their owners, insist on taking four hours' siesta in the middle of the day, which no arguments can induce them to dispense with, though, as I have before mentioned, their habits at other times are sufficiently active. No water being procurable, and the mosquitoes quite maddening, he rode off at last, leaving them with the peons, and came to ask us to help him. We first laughed at him, and then consoled him by explaining the habits of Cordovese sheep; and when it got a little cooler we all rode off together, and at last got his rebellious flock safely up to the estancia.

The usual time for shearing is about the beginning of November, but owing to the difficulty of procuring shearers this year, from the Indians being in the camp, we were forced to put it off till the end of December, and did not get everything finished till about the first week in January. We were tolerably satisfied with this first year's clip, though the value of wool had rather fallen during the last year; but we got as good a price for our long coarse wool in Frayle Muerto as was given in Buenos Ayres for the finest short wool, the market being quite overstocked with the latter article.

I forgot to mention that my brother and Hume brought with them another addition to our establishment besides themselves, in the shape of a large bull mastiff, just full grown, and a very valuable dog. Nell promised also to be a good guard -a very necessary thing in the camp, and for which the native dogs are not much to be depended upon. She was a most affectionate animal, and much beloved and respected during her residence with us, which was, alas! destined to be a very short one, as after a very few weeks she unfortunately followed us one very hot day when we were riding into Frayle Muerto, and before she got above halfway was so much affected by the heat, that she crept into the long grass and died there. We had got some miles before we saw her, or we should not, of course, have allowed her to come. A valuable dog like this was a great loss, as besides the expense of bringing her out from England, it was impossible to replace her in the country, where there are scarcely anything but curs. Of these we always had a large assortment of every possible size and shape, and who, though of no particular breed, were always ready to assist in any hunting that might be going on, in which they generally joined with more zeal than discretion. The best of the collection was a greyhound named 'Galgo', who was rather quick at catching deer. Frank also possessed a half-bred terrier called 'Spot', given him in Rosario, to which he was extremely partial, and which would attack foxes in the most intrepid manner possible. My own chief favourite was an old dog I had brought with me when first I went down to Monte Molino; he was named Cuatrojos (four eyes), a favourite native name for a dog, with a spot of tan over each eye. 'Chiña', a small white cur, was a great pet with everyone; and the whole pack, of course, walked in and out just as they liked, considering themselves entitled to the warmest and most comfortable place, and to everyone's first attention on all occasions. I usually found three or four faithful attendants reposing on my feet when I awoke in the morning.

My brother returned to us just about Christmas. He had got horses in Rosario, and ridden alone some seventy miles across the country, and had on the morning he reached us a most narrow escape of being drowned while crossing the Tercero, about six leagues from us. The river was very much swollen by the rains, and a tremendous current running. While swimming the two horses over, they became quite alarmed, and he, getting somehow or other entangled in the cord, found himself pulled off his horse, and struggling in a stream running like a mill-race, encumbered at the same time by a rope fastened to two frightened horses. Being a very good swimmer, he managed to keep up until he could free himself, and at last safely reached the shore; but swimming horses over a swollen river some eighty yards in width is rather a dangerous undertaking.

Shortly after this my brother received accounts from England, which made him feel at liberty to alter his previous intention of returning at once to England, and decided him on remaining with us, to try how he really liked a settler's life, for which in idea he had always had a great fancy. He therefore proposed to us to remain on for the present as a fourth partner, an offer to which we were all delighted to agree; and the new year found us with this addition to our numbers.

CHAPTER X.

CHOOSING THE SITE OF A NEW HOUSE - BRICK-MAKING - HORSE-RACING - HORSES OF THE COUNTRY; MODE OF BREAKING; THEIR COLOURS; HORSE DEALING.

We now began to make plans for building our new house, and determined to move to higher ground, nearer the river, as we thought it would be a better situation in many ways, and that a fresh spot could be better laid out for gardens, quintas, &c., than the place in which we were at present; but it was impossible to begin until the materials were got up to the place, as it was necessary to make all our bricks on the spot, and for this purpose we were also obliged to bring down wood from Frayle Muerto to burn them with.

The process of brick-making in the River Plate is a very simple one, and during its progress I was often reminded of the accounts in the Bible of the brick-making in Egypt. The following is a short description of the method pursued in the River Plate.

A well is first dug, and the grass cleared off a large space of ground, not far off from whence the earth is to be taken. Close to the well is made the pisadera, so called from pisar, to tread, in which the mud is to be trodden by mares, driven round and round by a man on horseback. The pisadera is a round enclosure of from six to ten yards in diameter, varying, of course, in size according to the number of workmen employed, as the mud hardens very quickly, and must be used while still moist. The pisadera is enclosed by posts with rails tied round, so as to keep the horses inside. It is first of all filled with earth to about two feet in depth, the earth being taken from the space already cleared, the soil being only used to about a foot in depth, that being as far as the black earth extends, the subsoil then becoming mixed with red sand, which, of course, is quite useless in brick-making. The water is drawn up by a horse in a large canvas bucket, and poured into the pisadera, until the earth seems sufficiently moistened. The horses are then turned in, and driven round and round until the cortador (brick-cutter) pronounces that it has reached the proper consistency for being formed into bricks. While this is going on, chopped grass, or straw if it can be obtained, is scattered over the composition in order to make the mild hold better together. A flat space of ground in the mean-time having been prepared close to the pisadera, for moulding the bricks, the mud when ready is wheeled out in barrows, and upset on a hide laid on the ground. The cortador has his wooden mould, which makes two bricks at a time, laid on the ground before him, and he raises up the mud on his arms, having clasped his hands together, and drops it into the mould; he then dips his hand into a bucket of water close by, and smooths over the surface, removing at the same time the superfluous clay, which he puts down close by, ready for the next pair of bricks; the mould is then raised by two handles on the outside, and wiped over with a wet rag before being used again, so as to prevent, the mud sticking to it; he pulls the hide after him as he moves along, placing the bricks in rows of from twenty to thirty pairs in length, on the flat space prepared for them.

One or two days, if the sun is at all hot, are quite enough to dry them sufficiently for setting up on edge, so that the other side way be dried. As they are turned all the edges are scraped smooth with a knife, and the under side pared flat. They are left for another day until dry enough to stack. Bricks dried in the sun like this are called 'adobes', and are much used for building, but, of course, are harder and better when baked, and for a large house one would never think of using 'adobes', but for any building of one story, out-buildings, &c., they answer very well; and, of course, it is a great advantage to be spared the expense of fuel, a dear article when one is forced to bring it all eighty miles in carts.

A good brick-cutter will often make over two thousand bricks in a day, some over three thousand, but this is very unusual; it is extremely hard work, and very tiring to the back, as one must stoop quite down to the ground to lift the mud on one's clasped hands, and the weight of earth thus raised is from thirty to forty pounds each time.

We contracted with a man to cut our bricks, and paid him about thirty shillings per thousand, also giving him and his peon beef and yerba. We all tried our hands at brick-making, and found it very tiring work, though I have occasionally made five hundred bricks in a morning; my brother soon gave in, saying his back was too long for the work.

The walls of houses, or enclosure walls, are often constructed of tapia, which is made in the following manner. A large wooden frame is put together, open at the top and bottom, measuring two yards in length, and about one in breadth. The surface earth slightly moistened is thrown into this separate layers, from three to four inches in depth, and well pounded with a huge wooden mallet until quite hard; another layer is then added, and so on until the frame is full. The frame is fastened together by wedges, which are then knocked out, and the base moved on to form the next brick, a large hard block being thus produced, which becomes almost as impenetrable as adobe.

The tapia is, of course, prepared on the spot intended for the wall, as each block weighing something like a ton, it would be almost impossible to move them, and their own weight keeps them firmly together, cement being quite unnecessary. Walls of a house are often begun by a layer of tapia, upon the top of which adobes or burnt brick can, of course, be built, the tapia forming a very solid foundation. Mud is used for mortar, and answers very well except for the foundation, and parts round the doors and windows, for which lime is employed; but as none is to be had nearer than Cordoba, settlers in the pampas are glad to dispense with it as much as possible.

The brick-making occupied several months, and in the meantime we indulged in the most magnificent plans for our future house. Walter was the chief architect, and threw himself into the business with his usual energy; indeed the accession of our two new partners enabled us to contemplate many improvements which would previously have been beyond our grasp; and both taking most sanguine views of the prospects of the country, roused us from the temporary depression which the late unfortunate Indian invasion had produced in the neighbourhood, and made us all set to work again with fresh vigour.

We also wrote home about this time, requesting to have a cook and gardener sent out to us, as we were heartily tired of acting in the former capacity ourselves, and soon heard that two Warwickshire men, one of whom I had known all my life, and who proved a most valuable acquisition to our party, were on their way out.

About this time the settlers in the camps round Rosario and Frayle Muerto, and in the north of Santa Fe, had determined to get up some English races, and the end of March had been fixed for the first general meeting, to come off at Roldan, a railway station just outside Rosario. In the previous September some races on a small scale had taken place, and we were all glad of such a good excuse for meeting friends and countrymen, which at the distance we all lived apart could not often be done.

Enough money had been raised for four good races, to be ridden by gentlemen riders, and managed on a different plan from the native races, which appear to an Englishman to he conducted on very singular principles. We all resolved to attend this first general gathering, two of us having been invited to act as stewards. Frank, Walter, and myself went down by train, but Hume and another friend who was staying with us resolved to ride down to Rosario, thinking that by this time they were Vaqueanos enough to find their way across the camp. They intended to pass the first night at a native estancia about sixteen leagues from us, not far from Cruzalta, a small village on the old post-road, between Saladillo and Rosario. They started off across the plain, and at length struck into a track leading, as they supposed, to Lobaton, where they intended to halt in the middle of the day, but after pursuing it for several hours still saw nothing but a boundless extent of flat green camp stretching away as far as the eye could reach. The time at which they ought to have arrived at Lobaton was long past, and they at length felt certain they had taken a wrong direction, and were wandering down towards the boundless deserts of the south. The only thing to be done was to retrace their steps, and ride back exactly as they had come, until they reached the spot where they first struck into the track, and where as they now felt convinced, they had turned to the south instead of to the north.

It may seem strange that such a mistake should occur, but no one who has not piloted his way over this monotonous country can imagine how little there is to guide a traveller when far away from all dwellings. At the time Hume and his companion took the wrong turn, it was about twelve o'-clock, and the sun was therefore no guide as to which direction they should pursue. They resolved to make the best of their way back, but after a little tine W. suddenly turned to Hume, saying he was so tired with the heat and want of water, that he could go no further, but must get off and rest for a short time. His companion remonstrated strongly against this, saying that their horses were already very tired, and if allowed to stop would become too stiff to go any further, in which case they themselves would be in considerable danger, as they had completely lost their reckoning as to where they were, and could only feel certain that it was many leagues from any human habitation, and they were entirely without water or provisions, both of which it was impossible to procure.

Upon this W. rode on for some distance, but at last became so faint from beat and fatigue that it was quite impossible for him to proceed; both therefore dismounted, and lay down on the ground close to their horses, who were almost as much in need of rest as their masters. W. instantly fell asleep; but Hume, who was less tired, lay awake, thinking over his position, nor were his reflections of a very cheerful nature. He was many miles from all possible help, his companion almost unconscious from exhaustion, and the horses likely to prove too tired to go a step further. Both were parched with thirst after their many hours' ride beneath a burning sun, and no water was to be procured. At one time he thought, as a last resource, of trying to shoot some of the deer that appeared in the distance, and of sucking their blood.

After about half-an-hour W. awoke, and told him he now felt able to go on. The horses were fortunately not too tired to move slowly, so remounting they jogged on. By this time it was near eleven p.m., and, the moon getting well up, they soon saw at a little distance what appeared to be a white mist, but proved, to their great delight, to be the Saladillo river. Men and horses drank eagerly of the somewhat brackish water, and, with a feeling of intense relief, prepared to pass the night on the bank of the river, heedless of mosquito bites and hungry stomachs. At daybreak they saw the village of Saladillo not a league off, and soon hitting off the 'tropa' road, which they had looked for so unsuccessfully the previous day, rode on to Lobaton, a wretched 'poblacion', consisting of three mud 'ranchos'. There they obtained some food, principally eggs and melons, but not having tasted anything for nearly thirty hours, they were not over fastidious. After this adventure they stuck to the post-road, avoiding any short cuts through the camp.

They reached Rosario safely, and told us their adventures; upon which we, after the manner of comforters, informed them that their misfortunes were all their own fault, for not taking our advice and sticking to the post-road; but they must have suffered a great deal from heat and thirst, as their faces were for some time quite blistered from the effects of the sun.

The races were a great success, the weather was beautiful, and a special train to Roldan was organised for the day. A good many ladies, both English and Spanish, were to be seen in the grand stand, which was very cleverly erected by the railway company upon trucks. The scene was a very novel and striking one, the gaily-dressed Gauchos galloping wildly about in the sunlight, which flashed upon the silver trappings of their horses, contrasting strongly with the grave black dresses of the gentlemen of the upper classes. Altogether it was a very cheerful and inspiriting sight.

The horses were all of the native breed on this occasion, though a great effort is now being made to introduce some English blood.

The day after the races a grand dinner was got up by all the English assembled in Rosario, and it was very pleasant to see all one's old friends again; we drank success to the Rosario Race Club, and to the English estancias in the River Plate. On the second day after the races we all returned by train to Frayle Muerto, Hume not caring for a second ride across the country; and found on reaching Monte Molino that all had been going on well, under the care of our worthy capataz Dan Mulligan. Lisada had left us a few weeks previously to set up on his own account at Frayle Muerto. He attended the races, an amusement to which he was very partial, bringing with him a certain celebrated Tordillo, supposed to have been an Indian racer, but it was not successful on this occasion. To console Lisada a little, I treated him to some champagne. It astonished him very much, but he pronounced it 'vino muy rico', a very excellent class of wine.

The horses in the River Plate were, as everyone knows, originally introduced by the Spaniards, though they have now become so perfectly indigenous that large troops of them are to be found towards the south in quite a wild state. They are small animals, from fourteen to fifteen hands in height, strong and wiry, and capable of doing a great deal of work on very little food; the number of miles they will travel in the day, when fed on nothing but grass, is very surprising, and I have known them do as much as seventy miles in this manner. Their usual pace is a slowish gallop, or else a sort of jog-trot, as they will not trot properly unless trained specially for the purpose. The way in which they are usually broken is very simple. The tropilla of horses is driven into the corral, and the colt intended to be broken is caught round the neck with a lasso, another lasso is then thrown round his forelegs, by means of which he is brought to the ground. His forelegs are then hobbled, and the recado, or native saddle, is girthed upon his back. A strip of hide is forced into his mouth, to act as a bit, to which a strong pair of reins are fastened; a firm bozal, or head-stall, is then put on, having a long soga, or rope of twisted hide, attached to it. The potro is then allowed to regain his feet, and the maneas, or hobbles, are taken of. The soga, which is perhaps twenty feet in length, is firmly held by a man, who allows the colt to gallop to the end of it, and then brings him up with a sudden jerk; after this has been repeated once or twice the domador prepares to mount. He first takes off his boots, ties a handkerchief firmly round his head, turns up his calzoncillas above his knees, so as to get a firm grip with his legs, and, while some one tightly holds the potro's head, springs into the saddle without touching the stirrups.

He then grasps the latter (which generally consists only of a sort of large leather button) between his great toe and the next one (a very painful operation to anyone but a Gaucho, by the way), and, having settled himself firmly, and made ready for a start, he calls out to his companions, 'Largue', let go. The colt will sometimes walk quietly off, as it too much surprised at finding some one on his back to make any resistance; but generally he starts off at a gallop, with his head nearly on the ground, backing so violently as to unseat any less-experienced rider. The domador, however, takes it very quietly, and sits quite firm through it all, flogging the horse violently the whole time, and sometimes also chastising him with heavy iron spurs, if he happens to be wearing boots and using a rather less primitive kind of stirrups. After half an hour's gallop the colt is brought back, partially subdued, and tied up for a few hours, when he receives a second lesson. This is continued for about a week, the horse being tethered, between times, to a long rope; at the end of this time he generally becomes tolerably tame; but some horses, of course, require a longer training. When he is considered sufficiently tame the heavy iron bit of the country is put into his mouth, and he is called a redamon, half-broken horse, until he is considered properly broken and will obey the reins; he is then called a cavallo. This very rough way of breaking-in is, of course, extremely bad for horses, spoiling both their tempers and their mouths, and generally making them timid, besides frequently laming them by the rough process of throwing them; and the English settlers now often break-in valuable colts themselves, preferring this to allowing the natives to maltreat them, as they almost invariably do.

The feeling between the Gaucho and his horse is not at all like that between the Arab and his steed, unless violent blows over the head, whenever the poor animal does not quite satisfy his master, are a proof of affection. Horses are never shod, except in the towns, as it is quite unnecessary out in the camp. There are a most curious variety of colours among the Argentine horses, quite unlike anything ever seen in Europe; they would be quite invaluable for Astley's, and indeed I believe some have been brought over for circuses. The natives, instead of giving names to their horses, always call them by their colours, the immense number of different shades preventing confusion; and they would speak of their tordillo, (grey), azuleco (blue, a sort of slate-colour quite unknown out of the Argentine Republic), colorado (red), and a hundred others. Some of the horses, if kept close to the house and kindly treated, will get very tame, and know their masters quite well. Horses have increased very much in value during the last few years. A very good horse could be bought for from 1l to 10ls. when I first went out, but now nothing worth having can be got under 3l.; and the natives, seeing that the English have money and are willing to pay, ask more of them than they would of one another; for anything unusually good they will ask as much as from 10l. to 15l. Mares, as a rule, are never ridden. There is quite as much trickery in horse-dealing in the River Plate as in other countries; and the Indian invasions cause horses to change hands so frequently that one is rather liable to buy stolen animals. To guard against this all horses are marked, and no one has a right to sell a horse unless he can prove that the mark is really his own, or produce a paper, signed by some judge, to show that the horse is his property; and when one sells a horse it is necessary either to give the paper or put on a countermark, i.e. one's own mark a second time, and the buyer can then add his own brand. If these precautions are neglected, and the rightful owner turns up, the horse is obliged to be restored; and if, as is generally the case, the seller is not forthcoming the money is lost. New comers are not always aware of this rule, and my brother's delight at his first purchase of a South American horse was much damped by discovering, in the course of a few days, that he had bought a well-known racer, stolen by some one or other, and he was, of course, obliged to relinquish his steed to the rightful owner. Hume was also a little taken in during his first few weeks in the country; having one day to come out alone from Frayle Muerto, he got a horse from the post-house, upon which he started. After a few leagues his horse began to show symptoms of fatigue; and after getting him on a few miles further, by dint of violent flogging and spurring, the old mancaron* refused to move at all, and Hume was forced to dismount and walk, leading his exhausted steed. Walking in the Pampas is not very amusing, especially in the height of summer, and he several times put his revolver to the horse's head, feeling half inclined to revenge himself on the annoying animal, who followed quite at his ease, but refused to move a step when

* *mancaron*, old scrow

mounted; he reflected, however, that if he killed the horse he should be obliged to carry the saddle and bridle himself, and, restraining his wrath, after an exhausting walk of ten or twelve miles he at length reached Monte Molino, not in the best of humours. He sent the horse back by a peon; and the next time he was in Frayle Muerto went to the postmaster to relieve his feelings; and, his stock of Spanish being then small, took out his revolver to explain to the man how he had felt inclined to shoot the horse. The alarmed postmaster's guilty conscience made him suppose the revolver was intended for himself, and he instantly fled from the supposed assassin; and, let us hopc, profited by the lesson.

CHAPTER XI

DESCRIPTION OF NATIVE SADDLE AND DRESS - SAD DEATH OF TWO ENGLISHMEN - M.'S DANGEROUS ADVENTURE WITH THE INDIANS.

Before quitting the subject of horses in the River Plate, I ought, I think, to give a short description of the native saddle used by the Gauchos, as well as of the dress of the Gauchos themselves, which I believe I have not yet mentioned. The native saddle or recado is a great load to put on a horse; very often weighing more than sixty pounds, with all its component parts. It varies according to the taste or means of the owner. The great advantage it has over an English saddle is, that when anyone on a journey is provided with it good recado and poncho, he has always a bed ready when he stops for the night; most Englishmen, however, ride on an ordinary saddle, carrying their blankets rolled up in front, a recado not being comfortable unless one is wearing the native dress. The recado is made up of several saddle-cloths, or sheepskins, put next to the horse's back; above these come two caronas, of raw hide, and one of leather, stamped into patterns with a hot iron. The caronas are about four feet long, and two wide, with a division in the middle, so that they hang across the horse's back, with an equal part on each side. Above these comes the recado, which is, so to speak, the saddle itself. This is made of wood, covered with leather, with a sort of peak before and behind, or in many cases it is nothing but two long rolls of straw covered with leather, lying one along each side of the horse's back. The whole of this paraphernalia is made fast by a broad hide girth called the cincha. This is made of two parts, one of which goes across the top of the recado, and the longer part underneath the horse. The two parts, to the end of each of which is attached a strong iron ring, are then made fast by a strip of hide, called the correan. The horse can be girthed up very tight by this means, which is very necessary, as it is to a ring attached to the upper part of the cincha that the lasso is made fast, and from this ring carts are pulled, instead of from the collar. A horse cannot, of course get so much purchase from the girths as from the collar, and Englishmen, therefore, use the ordinary harness, but the natives still stick to their old-fashioned way, and all the native horse-carts are made with a single hole instead of with shafts. The mode of pulling by the cincha is, however, very convenient, as when anything that must be dragged alone, such as a heavy log, for instance, has to be moved, a horse is attached to the load, and the desired object is easily effected. Above the cincha comes the cojinillo, which is made of wool of any colour. For ordinary work two or three sheepskins are laid across the recado, and made fast by a narrow strip of hide called a cinchon. The cojinillo may, however, cost almost any price, according to the fancy of the rider; and on great days the natives appear with very handsome ones, and with recados mounted with silver, their stirrups, and large spurs, being also of the same metal. Above the cojinillo, a small piece of well-softened leather, such as the hide of a carpincho, or river-pig, or the skin of some small animal, such as a fox, biscacha, &c., is generally placed, and is called the sobre puesto.

A party of Gauchos on a feast day, or some great occasion, such as races, riding at the sortija, &c., is a very picturesque sight.

Riding at the sortija is a very favourite game with the natives on holidays, and is carried on in the following manner. A small ring is suspended by a thread, and the competitors, with a short stick in their hands, ride at it at full gallop, and try to carry off the ring on the point of the stick; this, of course, requires great skill, and a successful tilter is greeted with much applause, receiving a ring as the prize of his skill.

It adds greatly to the brightness of the scene to see the spectators with their gaily coloured shirts, and broad belts covered with silver dollars, long knives, and horse-trappings, some of them quite covered with silver, as they generally carry all their wealth about them. The native dress consists of a loose pair of calzoncillas, or drawers, worked at the bottom, and edged with fringe, above which is worn a garment called a chiripa, in shape like a shawl; the two ends of this are fastened with a sash round the waist, the middle part hanging down like a bag and forming a sort of very loose trousers. The chiripa, which may be made of any sort of materials, such as wool, cotton, alpaca, or cloth, is of bright colours, woven in stripes, but the kind generally considered the smartest is made of black cloth edged with scarlet, and looks very well over a pair of white calzoncillas, with a red shirt above it. Patent leather boots with red or green tops are worn on great occasions, but on ordinary days boots of untanned leather, made from the skin of the hind legs of a mare, are much used.

The hock forms the heel, and the leg is cut off just above the fetlock joint, so that when the skin has been cut through at the top of the leg, the whole of it can be drawn off like a glove. The hair is scraped off, and the boot rubbed by hand until it becomes almost as soft as kid. The toe is thus, of course, open, and can be sewn up if the wearer wishes, but a large brown toe is generally seen protruding. The boots have to be tied up above the calf with garters, as they do not fit closely.

As a Gaucho has no pockets in any of his clothes, he always wears a broad leather belt, called a tirador, with pockets in it, which contain all his necessaries - tobacco, paper for cigarettes, and a flint and steel; a long knife is stuck in behind; and with a handkerchief tied loosely round his neck, or round his head just below his hat, his boleadores tied in front of his saddle, or slung round his waist, and his lasso coiled up behind him, his costume is complete.

The boleadores, which are used for catching wild horses, ostriches, or deer, consist of two large balls of wood or stone, covered with hide, to which are attached two strips of hide of an equal length, varying from three to four feet; to the end of these two strips is fastened a third strip with a smaller ball at the end of it. This ball is held in the hand, the boleadores are swung round the head and thrown by the Gaucho when at full gallop, at the animal that is to be captured. The object is to strike the hind legs, when the pace at which the animal is going makes the balls swing round and round until the legs are tied tightly together, when the prisoner soon falls to the ground. Small balls of lead or iron are used for ostriches and deer.

It takes a great deal of practice to be able to catch a particular colt or mare out of a large troop of animals galloping close together.

The native dress is very comfortable in hot weather, and we often wore it in the camp; it has also the great merit of cheapness, and stands the many rough occupations a settler is forced to engage in, better than broadcloth and fustian.

During the time of our race meeting at Rosario a great damp was thrown over our enjoyment by the sudden arrival of news of the murder of two Englishmen, much liked by us all. They were brothers: the eldest, a man of good property, had only come out to the country for a visit, his health being delicate, and travelling recommended for it; but the younger was intending to settle somewhere in South America. They had both been travelling about the country for some time, and with two other companions had before had a very narrow escape from the Indians.

On this last occasion they had started up the country from Rosario with a number of mules, bought in Entre Rios, intending to sell them in the upper provinces. Mendoza and San Juan were at this time in a very disturbed state, and travelling there was really dangerous unless with an extremely strong party. All their friends had tried to dissuade them from the expedition, advising them to defer it till things were a little more settled, but they were determined to go, being both very courageous, and, as it unhappily proved, underrating the danger. They had nearly reached San Juan in safety, when about the middle of the day on which this sad event occurred, while riding on ahead in search of a good place to rest in during the heat, they suddenly came upon a party of montoneros, the name given to the inhabitants of the sierras, who are at all times rather turbulent, and were just then very active in the revolution that was going on. These men were seated round a fire taking mate, and invited the two brothers to join them, an invitation which they at once accepted, not in the least suspecting any treachery. While they were all sitting quietly together in this manner the montoneros suddenly turned upon them, and, in spite of a desperate resistance made by the two brothers, although they had been taken quite unawares, they were both killed, after having shot several of their cowardly assailants. A Frenchman who was with them was also left on the ground for dead, but being afterwards found by some friendly natives, recovered from his wounds, and made his way back to Rosario, where he related these sad particulars. Both brothers had many friends, and their untimely fate was a great shock to us all.

They had some months before had a most narrow escape from the following dangerous position.

In company with two other friends, they had started on in expedition towards the Indian territory lying to the south-west of the province of Cordoba, near the Andes, intending to try whether they could not commence a trade with the Indians. They took with them several mules laden with aguardiente (a strong coarse kind of spirit), meaning to exchange it for cattle. When near one of the southern passes to Chili they fell in with a party of Indians, who seemed quite friendly; they therefore gave them some presents, and told them their object. After staying a few days in the same place a great many more Indians collected, and encamped near, coming up constantly to ask for more spirits, which they at last refused to give, as they did not see much chance of getting any cattle in return. They now began to suspect they had got into a trap, and resolved to make their position as strong as possible. They were encamped close to a stream, upon rocky ground, with bushes near, and made as good a fortification as they could round their encampment, with rocks, bushes, and mule packs, and being well armed, they knew the Indians would not like to attack them. They reminded like this for about ten days, the Indians coming up constantly to demand spirits, &,c., which they refused to give. At night they could see their unwelcome neighbours squatting round their fires eating their disgusting supper of raw liver,* made palatable by little bits of salt; and their appearance in the firelight, smeared all over with blood, often quarrelling and fighting among themselves, was quite demoniacal The two Englishmen's position was becoming very unpleasant, as their provisions were gradually coming to an end, and it was impossible for them to get safely away. They were just meditating a desperate effort in a retreat on foot, the Indians having got hold of all their horses and mules, when one day, to their great joy, a Chilian officer with a company of soldiers suddenly appeared. The wily Indians, not liking the look of their firearms, yet being resolved to make something out of their prisoners, had sent across to the Chilian authorities to say that they had surrounded some Spanish spies. The Englishmen soon convinced the officer as to who and what they were, upon which he kindly offered them an escort across the Andes, obliging the Indians, on the threat of not allowing them to trade with the Chilians, to give up some of their horses and mules, with which they gladly quitted the spot. The Indians had expected a great feast at their departure, as from the reduced number of their mules they could not carry off much of the aguardiente, but to their great disappointment the Englishmen piled all the demajuanas (a large glass bottle covered with wicker and containing three or four gallons) in a heap, and set fire to them and their packs, not leaving the place until all were burnt.

Our enterprising neighbour, M., who, as I have before mentioned, had several times been down to Rio Cuarto to purchase sheep for the different settlers round Frayle Muerto, was just about to start on another expedition there. We commissioned him, therefore, to bring us up one hundred and fifty head of cattle to keep for our own consumption, our increased num-

* Raw liver is a great Indian delicacy, as they generally roast to rest of their meat, except when on the march, when they are content to eat it raw

bers making this quite necessary, as we did not wish to kill our sheep, and were too large a party to depend any longer on game, or the unmarked cattle we occasionally picked up that had escaped from the Indians. Rio Cuarto, lying as it did so far to the south, being about twenty leagues from Saucé, and situated on the frontier, was very subject to Indian invasions, a month very seldom passing without the inhabitants being favoured with a visit from them, as it was a great place for breeding horses, cattle, and sheep.

M., in one of his previous trips, caught sight of the Indians in the distance, as he was returning with some sheep. They were, however, so much occupied as either not to see, or not to care to attend to him. As soon as he saw them he drove his flock into a hollow, and waited there rather anxiously until they were out of sight. They passed at some distance, but not too far for him to see them clearly, and even hear their shouts. The peons who were with him had ridden off at the first alarm, and hidden themselves, leaving him to his fate.

He started on his present expedition about the beginning of March, and returned with the cattle after about a month's absence, having met with the following adventure. He safely reached Rio Cuarto, and had been there a few days, when about two hundred Indians made their appearance outside the town. The Comandante got together as many men as he could, about fifty or sixty in all, to go out against them, and M. determined to go also. They rode out to meet the Indians, M. and the Comandante being in front, but as soon as they were within four or five hundred yards of the enemy, who were galloping down towards them, they suddenly perceived, on looking round, that all their soldiers had turned, and were making a rapid retreat to the river, on the other side of which was the town. Being only two against two hundred, they were, of course, obliged to follow their example; both, happily, were well mounted, and soon overtook their flying squadron, and no persuasion being able to prevail upon them to turn and face the enemy, it became a case of sauve qui peut. The river, from which the town takes its name, was about a mile off, and they made for it as fast as they could. The banks here were in most parts eight or ten feet high, and there were only one or two places where it was possible to ride down to the water. Below the barranca (bank) was a space of some hundred yards or so, before the water, of very rough and uneven ground. M., finding he was hardly pressed by the Indians, instead of making for the place where he could ride down, jumped over the bank, two men close to him having had their throats cut, their heads being nearly severed from their bodies; not a very pleasant sight, especially as he might judge what his fate would be if overtaken. The Indians, however, seemed unwilling to come to extremities with him, not liking the look of his revolver, which he kept in his hand, as a last resource, being resolved to sell his life as dearly as possible. After jumping down the barranca, his horse put his foot in a hole, and, rolling over, pitched him off over his head, and broke away from him down to the river. He now thought it was all over with him, but the Comandante called out to him to hold on to his stirrup-leather; and in this way both reached the water, where M. caught his horse, and remounted, and both crossing to the other bank, were soon in safety, as several men had come down there with rifles, ready to defend the bank, at which sight the Indians retreated, having killed some five or six soldiers in the way I have mentioned. After this they returned to their own territory, but a dreadful retribution awaited them on the way, as having to pass close by Rio Quinto, another small town on the frontier, the Comandante of that place sallied out with a strong body of men, and surprising the Indians in a hollow, while asleep, managed to kill some fifty or sixty of them, besides recapturing all the cattle and mares that they were carrying off with them. M. returned from this dangerous expedition about the end of March.

CHAPTER XII

FIRST APPEARANCE OF CHOLERA - CATTLE-MARKING - SALADERO - RUNAWAY ANIMALS.

During the summer which had just come to an end, the cholera had made its appearance, for the first time, as far as I am aware, in the River Plate, and had been very prevalent both in Rosario and Buenos Ayres. It was supposed to have come down the river from the allied forces engaged in the Paraguayan war, who had been suffering very severely from disease, occasioned by bad food and exposure to damp. These constant attacks of cholera and fever had more than decimated the army, and great fears were of course entertained as to the havoc that such an epidemic as cholera might make in the towns. The natives, and especially the lower class of them, who live in small filthy ranchos on the outskirts of Rosario, had been the chief sufferers, and hardly any cases of cholera had appeared among the foreigners and better fed natives.

Our well-known and popular consul, Mr. Hutchinson, exerted himself in the most devoted and praiseworthy manner to afford relief to the sick; and owing to his exertions a temporary hospital was erected, which was soon crowded with patients.

At the time of the races, the cooler weather having begun, the cholera abated; and there were no fresh cases until the following summer, when it again raged, with much greater violence.

Upon our return to Monte Molino, immediately after our pleasant race meeting, we found that M. had just arrived with the cattle from Rio Cuarto. As part of them were for our neighbours at Monte de la Lèña, we at once let them know of their arrival, that they might come over with their peons as soon as possible, to separate their own cattle from ours, and to mark them.

Cattle-marking in South America is one of the great events of the year, and is, I think, one of the most exciting incidents connected with a settler's life. Many persons have probably read accounts of cattle-marking in other books, but a word or two on the subject may not, perhaps, be out of place here. The Australian cattle-marking is, no doubt, very exciting sport, and requires great skill and nerve, but the picturesque-looking Gaucho, whirling his lasso round his head, and throwing it with unerring aim, adds an indescribable wildness to the whole scene. The cattle are not usually confined in corrals, but are accustomed to come up every night on to the rodeo, a large bare spot where they sleep, and it is here that the branding takes place.

When the yearly marking is about to begin, notice is given to the neighbouring estancieros, that they may come over with their peons, to pick out any of their own cattle which may have joined the other herd. The cattle are driven up to the rodeo, and the peons then begin to catch the young beasts that are to be marked. One having been selected, the peon throws his lasso over its horns, no easy matter when a beast is young and has very short ones; but greater command can be obtained over the animal in this manner than by lassoing it round the neck. A very young calf, however, must, of course, be caught round the neck, as it has no horns. As soon as the beast is fast by the head, another peon rides up to him, and lassoes him round the hind legs -a much more difficult operation. He is then pulled up to the fire, where the branding irons are being heated; the two peons gallop in different directions, and the unfortunate beast is thrown heavily on his side. The men at the fire next seize him, and while one holds the head of the animal firmly, the other applies the red-hot brand, until the mark is sufficiently burnt in, when the lasso round the horns is cast loose. The animal is then allowed to rise, the lasso round the hind legs being kept tight until he gallops off in the direction of the herd, upon which the peon rides after him, and allowing the lasso to slacken, it soon falls off, and another victim is selected.

As we had only about two hundred to brand, we tied their legs, when they were pulled close to the fire, so that four or five could be marked before the iron got cold. They were then untied, and let loose. The last operation is not unattended with danger, when this little attention is paid to a bull who has had his temper ruffled by a good deal of previous driving, followed up by the soothing application of a red-hot iron. On this occasion, one of our peons, Manuel, having released a cow, laid himself down behind her, thinking that she would be glad to rejoin her companions. She turned, however, and commenced a violent assault upon him, tearing his shirt, and already somewhat dilapidated calzoncillos, and attempting to horn him. I galloped at her, to divert her attention, upon which she turned her attack upon my horse, who not being equally quick at turning, narrowly escaped getting a horn into his flank; but Manuel in the meantime made good is retreat, and got away only with a fright.

Horses when branded are, of course, thrown with greater care, and the operation takes place in a corral. Valuable horses are generally only hobbled, and receive the brand quietly.

At the finish up of a cattle-marking a great delicacy is provided for the peons -'carne con cuero', i.e. an animal roasted in its hide. This is considered an excellent dish, and when cold is especially good. The Gaucho is seen to great advantage on these occasions, his appetite being almost beyond belief.

Frank had a peon in Entre Rios who at a sheep-shearing has been known to devour a whole sheep. Not wishing to be regarded as a second Munchausen, I may as well add that our active sheep do not weigh quite as much as those who have led a contemplative life in English fields.

Cattle-breeding, when the land is fitted for it, is one of the most paying concerns in the whole country; and our estate being particularly suitable for the purpose, from the abundance of rich pasture and constant supply of water, it was very trying to be prevented from engaging in it, on any considerable scale, by the constant fear of Indians; but we still look forward to a halcyon time, when Indians shall be unknown in the land, and countless herds seen round Monte Molino.

The great markets for cattle are, of course, the Saladeros, which are situated on the outskirts of all the larger towns, and where the cattle are handed over by their owners to the proprietors of these establishments.

At the risk of repeating what has been better told before, I must here add a short account of what I have myself seen at a saladero in Buenos Ayres. The cattle are often brought in from a great distance - frequently as much as fifty or sixty leagues - at a tremendous pace, and so do not, as may be imagined, arrive in a very fat condition. They are driven into a large pen, having an entrance made out of it into a smaller pen, shaped like a funnel. A sufficient number of animals to fill the smaller pen are urged into it, and the work of destruction then begins. The chief executioner, or capataz, stands on a raised platform at the side of the pen, with a thick lasso in his hand, one end of which runs through a pulley, and is then attached to the girths of two mounted horses. The capataz then throws the lasso round the horns of one or two animals, and calls out to the horsemen, who start off at a sharp pace, hauling the captured beasts to the narrow end of the pen. He also then walks to the end of the pen, stoops over, and with a sharp knife piths the animal, that is, just divides the spinal cord. The victim drops dead upon a truck, which is waiting to receive his body, the lasso is slipped off the horns, and the truck, which runs on a tramway, hauled under a long shed, the carcase being there rolled off, and the truck immediately pushed back ready for the next subject. The throat of the dead animal is cut, to let the blood out, and the skin stripped off, almost by magic. The limbs are then cut off, and all the meat cut from the body, in thin slices, which are wheeled away to the salting-house, where they are placed in alternate layers of meat and salt. After the meat has remained in this state for some time, it is taken out, and hung up to dry, after which it is piled in large stacks, until shipped off to the Brazils and West Indies, where great quantities are consumed by the black population, negroes being, apparently, the only people able to eat it. It has been tried in England, but was not much relished there, which I do not much wonder at, as it is anything but tempting in appearance. The process of catching, killing, skinning, and cutting up the animal, takes less time than I have taken to describe it in, for I have timed one of the skinners, who, from the time the animal was brought into the shed until he was skinned and his four legs cut off, was not five minutes at his work. It is simply wonderful to watch the rapidity with which their knives go, and they never seem to cut a hole in the hides, for if they do, a certain amount is deducted from their wages for each cut made. The bones are boiled down in huge boilers, in order that the fat may be extracted from them; and they are then either burnt for bone-ash or shipped whole to be used in England or other countries; the hoofs and horns, of course, being also kept and made useful.

On the whole, the aspect of a saladero, as may be imagined, is not a very pleasant one, but it is a sight that ought to be seen by every traveller in the River Plate. At some of the largest of these establishments, over a thousand head of cattle are slaughtered in a day; and as there are a good many saladeros at work for several months in the year, one may realise what thousands of animals are killed annually. Mares are also destroyed, in the same wholesale manner, for their fat, bones, and hides; but a restriction has been put upon the mare-killing business, from a reasonable fear that horses might become scarce if such large numbers of mares were slaughtered. Crowds of fierce-looking dogs may be seen snarling and growling at each other, contending for the scraps of offal, at the saladeros; and gaunt, hungry pigs also abound, but their appearance is quite sufficient to make one shun pork carefully in Buenos Ayres. It is quite as well to arm oneself with a stick or whip when on a visit to one of these establishments, to keep off the attacks of dogs, who are apt to fly at one's legs. The chief workmen in the saladeros seem to be Basques, from the Pyrenees, of whom there are a very great number in Buenos Ayres, as well as in the camp, where they make very good shepherds, and work hard and steadily. The smell of the salting-houses is not very agreeable, and in the town of Buenos Ayres itself, when the wind blows from Barracas, where they are situated, the stench is insufferable, especially when the bones are being burnt for bone-ash, but it is said to be very wholesome. We made a party of five or six to go down to see the saladeros, as time is apt to hang rather heavy on hand in Buenos Ayres.

A railway now runs from the town to the Boca, the port from which all the salted meat, &c., is shipped; but at the time of which I am speaking it was not finished, and we went down to Barracas (a store) by diligence. Many attempts have been made to prepare the meat properly for exportation; and, if this could be done, no doubt very large fortunes might be made; but one can hardly expect meat to be worth much, when the animals killed are so tired that they can hardly move, and have little or no fat on them.

Liebig's extractum carnis is, however, very good, and there is no doubt that, in a short time, some better plan for preserving meat will be found out, so that it will become much cheaper in England.

Señor Sarmiento, who is now the president of the Argentine Republic - a very clever and enlightened man, to whom we confidently look for many reforms - has offered a large reward to anyone who can find out a really successful method for salting or otherwise preserving beef, so that it may be fit to be imported into England. Australian beef, as my readers know, is now sent to England in great quantities, and why not South American?

A new scheme has been started for bringing live stock to England, and the monopoly granted by the Argentine Government to an English gentleman, a friend of mine, who is the chief mover in the matter. And, if it can be made to pay, it will, of course, be a source of great wealth to the speculators; but time alone can show the result.

We may, however, reasonably expect to be able to compete with the Australians, in bringing preserved meat to England from the River Plate, our greater nearness to home being so much in our favour.

Just after we had finished our cattle-marking,- the animals from Rio Cuarto not having arrived in very good condition for killing, and we being rather short of meat - Hume and one of the Monte de la Lèña party, who also wanted to buy a few beasts for the same purpose, went over together to a small cattle estancia on the banks of the Rio Tercero, between Saladillo and Frayle Muerto. There they picked out a few fat bullocks, which Hume and a peon who was with him got safely up to Monte Molino, arriving in the evening from Monte de la Lèña, where he had passed the previous night, so as to bring the beasts home slowly. We fastened them, as we thought, safely into the corral, securing the entrance, according to custom, by placing several large wooden bars across it; but when we went to inspect our new purchases, at daybreak, they were nowhere to be seen, having broken out of the corral and made their escape.

We guessed that they had returned to their former abode, as cattle and horses have always to become querenchiados, that is, accustomed to one place, before they will take to it; and, when bought and transferred to a distance, they will, unless looked sharply after by day and shut up at night, return to their former home. Hume, therefore, again started off in pursuit of the runaways, and found them, as he expected, at their old residence, about eight leagues off; he could tell, by tracing them, that they had made their way quite straight across the camp, instead of returning by Monte de la Lèña, the round-about road by which they had come, exercising a curious instinct, which they seem to possess in common with dogs and cats, and showing themselves better vaqueanos than some of their owners, the latter only acquiring this power after a long residence in the country. Hume brought them back, and they were again shut in, and this time with more precaution than before. The next morning they had again vanished, having on this occasion, as they were unable to break through the bars, actually leapt or scrambled over a height of five or six feet. A third time they were brought back, and it was only by keeping a constant guard over them for several days that we were at last able to retain them.

After these constant gallops across the Pampas they were not much stouter than the Rio Cuarto herd. It is better, when buying a quantity of cattle, to bring them from a long distance, as they will not then attempt to return to their former querenchia.

CHAPTER XIII

WE BEGIN TO BUILD OUR HOUSE - ILLNESS - I GO TO LAS ROSAS AND BUENOS AYRES - PATAGONES AND PATAGONIANS - CIVILISED ESTANCIAS - BUENOS AYRES RACES - DEPARTURE OF FRIENDS FOR EUROPE.

The cattle-marking being now happily concluded, we turned all our attention to our new house. The brick-making had gone on vigorously all this time, and a well had been sunk close to the spot we had chosen for building on. This new site was a mile from the iron house, and, of course, the move seemed a great pity in many ways, as all the ditches, enclosures, &c., had to be made over again, and we lost the benefit of our montecito (small group of trees), there not being a vestige of anything taller than a blade of grass on the new site. On the whole, however, we felt we should do better to move, in spite of all these objections, as the much nearer neighbourhood of the river would be an immense advantage, and it would also serve as a boundary on one side to our new enclosures, which we intended to begin on a much larger scale. The newly-chosen spot was also higher ground than our first settlement, and would, therefore, give us a better view of the country, which the possibility of Indian attacks made a great desideratum. Having fully resolved on the move, we determined to lose no time in making it.

I was, however, obliged to leave my companions to do most of the work, being laid up with a slight attack of illness, and though just able to get about, it was in a feeble sort of way. An invalid in the camp is rather a miserable being. I don't know how gipsies may feel when ill, but I can say, from experience, that a sick settler is certainly not a person to be envied. I had been ill about a week, and was lying on my bed in the iron house, rather late one evening, when, the house-door being partly open, which, indeed, was its normal state, some four-footed creature suddenly rushed in and concealed itself under my bed, having just excited a tremendous commotion as it passed the dogs, by biting a small puppy who was curled up in an inoffensive manner, no way provoking any attack. The whole indignant pack rushed at the intruder, who was shortly despatched; and, his corpse being extracted from beneath my bed, he proved to be a fox, who was most likely prowling about in search of a stray cock or hen, the South American foxes being quite as partial to poultry as the English ones.

We kept his skin as a memento of the circumstance, but these kind of incidents not being very favourable to the recovery of a patient, my companions strongly pressed me to go down to Rosario for better advice and more comfortable nursing than could be had in the camp; which, after a vain endeavour to shake off the attack without leaving home, I at length did. My brother accompanied me, and I was soon comfortably lodged in the Hotel de la Paz. Here my illness turned to a sort of fever, which kept me for about a fortnight in bed, and the worst being then over, I was soon well enough to get out to my friends at Las Rosas, where every care was taken of me, and I led a luxurious life. I had been here a few days when a neighbouring estanciero arrived from Rosario, and informed me that he had come up in the train with two Englishmen, who were on their way to Monte Molino, and whom I, of course, knew to be the gardener and cook that we had for some time been expecting from Warwickshire. I was very glad to hear of their having reached Rosario safely, and a few days later to receive letters from my brother announcing their arrival, having felt a little anxiety as to how they would manage their journey up the country.*

Don Pepe, who knew the were coming, received them at the fonda, and put them in the way of getting horses and a guide to our estancia. They were also, I believe, welcomed at the fonda by our old assistant, Jack the second, who passed much of his time there when his finances admitted of it; indeed, he was generally known in Frayle Muerto by the name of El chupador, the meaning of which I leave to my intelligent readers to discover. In some of his lucid moments, I imagine, he made out who the newcomers were, and interpreted Don Pepe's directions to them. Jack had by this time finally quitted us, as we really could not put up with him any longer. I was still at Las Rosas when rumours not particularly calculated to cheer a convalescent reached me, of the Indians having been up to Monte Molino, and having again swept off most of our horses. This intelligence made me rather anxious, until I got letters from my brother a few days later, telling me that the Indians had really been again in our neighbourhood, but

*see note at the end of the chapter

that we had this time escaped a visit from our old friends. Our neighbours at Monte de la Lèña had, however, not been so fortunate, and when I saw James W. a little later, he gave me the following account of his first sight of the Indians.

The new azotea (house) at Monte de la Lèña was now complete, and besides the usual occupants, T. had invited a young Englishman and his wife, lately arrived in the country, to stay with him until they had some better place to take a lady to than the fonda in Frayle Muerto.

On the eventful morning in question B. was the first stirring in the house, and while dressing, just at daybreak, chanced to look out of thc window, when he suddenly perceived a number of men surrounding the house. He instantly called up the rest of the party, who, of course, saw at once that the intruders must be Indians, and having snatched up the first weapons within reach, they all mounted to the roof of the house, from whence they proceeded to fire upon the invaders. The Indians had, however, by this time begun to retreat, driving of with them most of the horses, and none of the shots took effect. The whole scene must have presented rather a ludicrous appearance had there been any spectators sufficiently unconcerned to be amused at it; and James W., while telling me about it, laughed a good deal at the recollection of the besieged party, vcry lightly arrayed in the first articles of clothing that had come to hand, sitting shivering on the roof, in the grey dawn of a very cold morning, watching their property rapidly disappearing in the distance.

Nothing had been seen or heard of the Indians at Monte Molino when James W. galloped over there in the afternoon, to see how his neighbours had fared, and to relate his own losses; and nothing further was seen of them for several months by any of the settlers, as after the attack on Monte de la Lèña they made the best of their way back to their own territory.

I stayed on at Las Rosas until nearly the end of June, and being still weak, in spite of all the care and kind nursing I received under K.'s hospitable roof, I resolved to go down to Buenos Ayres, and try what that salubrious place would do for me. I established myself at the Universelle, a casa amueblada next door to the Bolsa; and when so minded, could amuse myself in the afternoon by watching the mercantile world of Buenos Ayres collect outside for business. After about six weeks I began to feel the good effects of the change, and was able to enjoy the kind hospitality of various friends.

There was no opera company in Buenos Ayres until just the end of my stay, but I consoled myself with frequent visits to the French theatre, where the performance was very passable.

I one day received a ticket from a kind Buenos Ayrean friend for a very interesting entertainment in the Colon theatre. All the free schools in the province of Buenos Ayres were assembled to receive their prizes, which were given away in the presence of crowds of spectators; the enormous opera-house, one of the largest in the world, being filled in a way that would have astonished and delighted the most sanguine of managers. There were several hundred children, all dressed in white and blue, and it was a very pretty sight to see them walk gravely up to receive their medals, their large dark eyes, the characteristic beauty of Spanish children, sparkling with delight.

Early in August I was pressed to accompany some friends on an expedition to Patagones, a new settlement on the Rio Negro, some hundred leagues to the southward of Buenos Ayres, and thinking the sea voyage would complete my cure, I agreed to go with them. The Rio Negro was a short time ago supposed to divide the province of Buenos Ayres from Patagonia, but the Argentine Government now claim part of Patagonia as their property, and sell land to anyone who likes to buy it. The town of Patagones is on the southern side of the Rio Negro, and at no very great distance from Bahia Blanca, a small town close to the sea. The settlement has only been formed very recently, and but little was known about it, but that little was so favourable, that my friends, who had as yet no place of their own, were anxious to see it before deciding where to settle. Patagones is supposed to be remarkably well fitted for agriculture, and as the harbour is good, Buenos Ayres offers an excellent market for the crops grown there; the Indians in this part are also at present quite friendly to the settlers, which I could not honestly say was the case with my own dark-skinned neighbours. My intended voyage, however, fell to the ground, as the steamer which plies to and from was long delayed at Patagones by bad weather, and when she did at last reach Buenos Ayres it was in a state which required repairs before she was again fit for sea. I could not then afford any longer delay before returning to Monte Molino, so was compelled to give up the expedition. My friends started for Patagones a few days before I left Buenos Ayres, and were so favourably impressed with the place, that three of them bought land there, and are, I believe, getting on very well.

Another Patagonian colony had been previously founded by some Welshmen, at a place called Chupat, a good deal farther south, but it was a complete failure, and provisions ran so short that but for timely aid from the English ships stationed in the River Plate all the settlers would have been staved to death. The place is quite abandoned now, most of the colonists having moved to Patagones, and the rest are dispersed through the River Plate country.

My curiosity about Patagonia had lately been a good deal increased by frequently seeing some specimens of its inhabitants, who had come at this time to Buenos Ayres to make some agreement with Government about land. These envoys, to the number of about ten or twelve, were to be seen constantly in all parts of the town, where they excited a great deal of interest. The really were on a much larger scale than ordinary mortals, the tallest of them measuring six feet eight inches in height, and sixty inches round his chest. They had large flat faces, and very high cheekbones, with long black hair hanging over their shoulders, but no beard or whiskers, these ornaments not being bestowed by nature on any of the South American Indians. Altogether the Patagonians were as unprepossessing specimens of humanity as could well be seen. On their first arrival they wore their native dress, a robe of guanaco skins (thc guanaco is a sort of llama, very common in the south), but they soon assumed the Gaucho dress, and conformed in many ways to civilised habits. They all understood Spanish, and one of them could speak a little English, but this accomplishment, I believe, he had picked in from the missionaries in his own country, and in spite of this convincing proof 'that the creature had glimmerings' as Andrew Fairservice would have said, they all had a very stupid look, and struck one as belonging to a very low order of mortals.

The chief topic of interest in Buenos Ayres was, of course, the Paraguayan war, which was just then at its height, and, indeed, struck one as only likely to terminate in the same manner as the celebrated battle between the two Kilkenny cats, General Mitré, who was our president, being determined to crush Lopez, and the latter appearing equally determined not to give in, a resolution which the natural strength of the country and the determined bravery of his troops enabled him at present to carry out. The war drained the country of men and money, and was the real cause of the undefended state of the frontier, so that we all looked forward impatiently to its termination; it continued, however, with undiminished force for another two years; but, from accounts recently received, I trust the apparently endless struggle is now about to terminate.

A short time before I returned to Frayle Muerto I was invited to pay a visit to an estancia, about eighteen leagues to the south of Buenos Ayres. It belonged to an Englishman, and I was much edified by beholding the comfort to which estancieros may hope to attain. Los Sajones was a great contrast to our dwellings in the camp, and far ahead even of the much-envied Las Rosas; but it was, of course, a long-established place, and as safe from Indians as a villa at Richmond. The house, which was, of course, azotea (one-storied), according to the fashion of the country, was large and comfortable, built round a half-square, the inside surrounded by a verandah, over which, beautiful creepers hung in the greatest profusion; there was a delightful garden, and the whole place was surrounded by quantities of trees of every description, a luxury which can be properly appreciated by no one who has not dwelt for some time on the treeless waste of the Pampas. A large party were assembled in the house, as some races were shortly to be held in the neighbourhood; and we spent our time, just as in any country-house in England, between riding, crôquet, and dancing; a dance was given at an estancia about three miles off, to which we all went, and one, in return, was soon after got up at Los Sajones.

The races went off very well, and we drove to them in a large waggonette, much as we might have done to Ascot or Epsom, and in a very different way from Hume's wild ride across the camp to Roldan; but when we reached the racecourse at Jeppner the scene was not very different from the Rosario races; and an English frequenter of the turf would have been rather astonished at the wild-looking Gauchos, galloping madly about in every direction, and shouting as only a native South American can shout.

A few days after the races I returned to Buenos Ayres, and found letters from Monte Molino awaiting me, with the information that Hume was obliged to return home at once, in consequence of letters he had just received from England, and that in a very few days he would be in Buenos Ayres, where he hoped to see me before sailing.

Several other of our chief friends were going home at the same time for a few months' holiday; Charlie T., James W., and our friend M.; the latter not only intending to take a short holiday, but also to bring a steam plough back with him, as he thought it would pay well to introduce it into the country. I was, of course, very sorry to lose Hume, but hoped he would not be absent very long.

Besides the unwelcome intelligence of the departure of so many friends, my letters informed me of the arrival of a new companion, whom we had been expecting for some little time. J. was an old friend and neighbour at home, and, having taken a great fancy for a settler's life, was coming to us, to learn a little of the camp ways, before setting up for himself, as he had only just left school, and as yet knew but little of farming. He was, as may be easily imagined, a very welcome addition to the party, but, like G., did not at first join us as a partner.

In a few days the four homeward-bound travellers appeared. Hume brought me very good accounts of affairs at Monte Molino, telling me that the new house had gone on so rapidly as to be nearly completed; he gave me a long list of things wanted for the place - furniture, stores, &c. - all of which could be got better and more cheaply at Buenos Ayres than elsewhere; and, the list being as long as those of commissions from friends in the country usually are, my last week at Buenos Ayres was pretty well filled.

My friends soon secured their passages on board the La Place, one of the Liverpool steamers just about to sail. We all dined together the evening before they started, and the next day I and several other friends, not so happy as to be homeward-bound, went on board to take leave of the departing settlers; after an affectionate farewell, we descended into our boat and sailed back to the mole, watching the La Place slowly steaming away into the distance, with many wishes for her safe voyage, and not a few that we were also on board her bound for Europe.

NOTE.- *The following extracts from the letters of one of these men to his friends at home may help to give my readers a clearer impression of the resources of the country; and while showing the paradise which such a country is to labouring men, at all events to those recently arrived from England, they also show that if well used it may fairly be regarded as 'a land of promise' to their masters: - 'This is a fine country for living; plenty of beef and mutton, and fowls, ducks, and turkeys; beef and mutton from one penny to two pence per pound. I often think of the poor people in England when I see the meat being kicked about steets, or a great dog dragging a piece of beef or mutton about enough to dine twenty people'.*

- 'This is a very nice place, about 25,000 acres of most beautiful soil, very level ground, and six miles of river frontage. The river, I must tell you, is quite covered over with birds. Swans, geese, ducks, and other beautiful birds too nu-

merous to mention. Thousands and thousands of each sort; when yon frighten them up they make such a noise you can scarcely hear one another speak, and out in the camp there are hundreds of wild deer'.

- 'The soil is beautiful; I can dig as much before breakfast here as in a whole day in England'. -'You would like to see us sometimes picking ducks, geese, swans, and snipe; you would think it was not much like starving to see ten or fifteen ducks cooked at once; and I can assure you they are beautiful ones too, some as large as the English tame ones, and as fat as they can be. I am sorry to tell you the swans have done laying now; and we shall get no more eggs for a fortnight, until the ducks and geese and other water fowls begin, then we shall get thousands. It is a strange thing, the swans' eggs are no stronger tasted than the English hens' eggs'. -'I only wish I had been here years before; it is a fine country for working men to come to, there are so many good things to be had. We can get any quantity of eggs, &c. I went the other day to get a few for breakfast, and brought a pock basketful. There is one thing I cannot quite manage, and that is to eat one whole ostrich egg; it is too much for me, although I am so fond of them. They are beautiful eggs; we have about one hundred a week of them, this last four or five weeks'. -'I must tell you about my horse-dealing. I have bought three. The three cost me 2l. 12s; one is three years old, another four, and the other aged; one turned out to be s stolen one, and after I had it about a month the man who owned it came for it'. -'We have a nice bed of melons, cucumbers and vegetable marrows. I dare say it will surprise you when I say we are going to plant twenty or thirty acres of vegetable marrow this year for the pigs; and I must not forgot to tell you that we have some radishes in the garden eighteen inches long and twenty inches round. I never saw such monsters in my life before; they are from some of the seed I had from Day's at Alcester'.

CHAPTER XIV

ARRIVAL OF RAMS - RETURN TO FRAYLE MUERTO - PLEASANT NEWS FROM HOME - RETURN TO MONTE MOLINO.

A short time before this we had written to England for some rams, being very anxious to try whether, by crossing our sheep with some good English rams, we could not get a superior class of wool. Eight long-woolled sheep, Cotswold and Leicester, had accordingly been despatched from Liverpool, and, a few days before my departure from Buenos Ayres, I heard of the arrival of the Galileo, by which ship they were to come. This was very fortunate, as I could myself superintend their landing, and, as I was just going to return to Monte Molino, could look after them on their journey, there being several changes to makc by the way. I accordingly got a boat, and went off with a friend to the Galileo. The day was very rough, and we were more than four hours getting out to the steamer, but found, when we got on board, that the eight rams were all in excellent health and condition. There was a prosperous British look about them all; the Cotswold, especially, might have served for the sign of the golden fleece; and they formed rather a contrast to the spare sheep of the Pampas, who too frequently bear a striking resemblance to woolly greyhounds.

Charlie T. was also expecting some rams, and eight had been sent out to him; but he had not been so lucky as ourselves, two of his number having died on the voyage, and two more were looking very ill. We, however, got the six survivors safely ashore with my eight, as I had promised Charlie that I would look after them for him; and they were all housed at some stables for a few days, until the steamer was ready to start for Rosario. The two sick rams shortly followed their companions, in spite or all I could do for them; but, the twelve others having been put on board one of the river steamers, I bid adieu to my kind friends, and started for

Rosario with all my belongings, which, indeed, were considerable, as they included all the commissions sent from the estancia.

I found my brother at Rosario, come down to purchase timber and other materials necessary for completing the house. After three days' halt there I proceeded by train to Frayle Muerto, leaving Walter to complete his purchases, and taking with me a quantity of timber that he had besides the rams, stores, &c., delivering the four surviving sheep to Gerald T., who had now finally left our neighbourhood and established himself at his new estancia, about eight leagues to the north-west of Las Rosas.

I was accompanied by four or five friends, lately arrived in the country, who were anxious to see the camps round Frayle Muerto, before deciding where to settle. I had, therefore, asked them to come out with me, as our shearing was soon coming on, and there was a great deal of other work going forward, which would give them a fair idea of what life in the camp was like. On reaching Frayle Muerto we found that the river was very much swollen, and the old floating bridge washed away, so that the only means of getting our goods across was in a small raft, on which only a light load could he placed.

The railway company were putting up a bridge for Government, but, unfortunately for us, it was then only in course of construction. It was to be a suspension bridge, with a span of about eighty yards in width; and when finished, some six months later, proved to be a great comfort and convenience, not only to the town, but to all the settlers round Frayle Muerto, as crossing everything on rafts was both a tedious and expensive process.

The weather was very hot, and I was exceedingly glad of the assistance. of my friends, who were soon initiated into the ways of the country, and worked away with their greatest zeal. The rams were, of course, conveyed over first, and safely lodged in a little shed at the fonda, where I had them shorn, as their fleeces had got very long, and they began to feel the heat a good deal. I sent off a chasqui (messenger) to Monte Molino directly I arrived, for our carts, desiring them also to send over horses for myself and my friends.

After three days' hard work, we got everything across the river; but it was rather a fatiguing business, as the station was more than half a mile from the river, and everything had to be loaded and unloaded between the station and the raft, and after being ferried across, had again to be placed in carts, which deposited their load at the fonda, there to await the arrival of our own carts. In addition to this, the banks of the river were extremely steep, so that carrying everything up and down them was no joke. At last, however, I happily completed my toils, and we were all resting at the fonda, awaiting our carts, the horses having been brought by the chasque, on his return, when one of our peons suddenly entered the room, and greeted me with the following pleasing news: '¿Cómo le va, Don Ricardo? Me alegro mucho de verlo tan bueno. Los Indios han llevado todos los cavallos y la hacienda de Monte Molino'.* He had been despatched by Frank with this cheering intelligence, and soon proceeded to give me the following account, interspersed with many wishes respecting the future destiny of the Indians, more heartfelt than benevolent.

The day after the chasque had started with the horses, Frank, J., and a friend who was staying with them, had gone to the new house, to put up wire fencing round a large paddock, of about a hundred and fifty acres, that was just being enclosed, and which stretched from the house down to the river. They were working away very happily, never dreaming of an attack, when one of the peons galloped up, calling out to them that the Indians had driven away all the cattle. They at once jumped upon their horses, and soon reached the iron house, but only in time to see the Indians disappearing in the distance.

Had they happened to have been up at the house, they would certainly have saved some of the stock, as they could easily have beaten off the marauders, the number of Indians who actually drove off the cattle being but small, the main body of them, about two or three hundred in number, remaining only just in sight, at a great distance.

Fate was certainly against us on this occasion, as in consequence of its being a very windy day, the bricklayers were unable to work at the new house. Had they been there as usual, they must from their elevated position have seen the Indians a long way off, and would have given notice of their approach in time for the animals to have been driven up to the corrals, and a defence properly organised. As it was, there was unfortunately no one at the iron house to take the lead in a sortie. Frank and his two companions must have had a very narrow escape of an encounter, as the Indians must have passed within half a mile of the place where they were working, but the nature of the ground prevented their seeing the depredators, and the violent wind carried their shouts in a different direction.

*'How do you do, Don Ricardo? I am much pleased to see you so well. The Indians have carried off all the horses and cattle from Monte Molino'.

Henry, one of our new workmen from England, was constructing, a shed for the rams, and saw the Indians, when at some little distance, but thought they were only some natives running mares. He had been but a short time in the Pampas, and though doubtless he had heard plenty of stories of the Indians from our capataz Dan, it never entered his head that they were now before him. As it was, the invaders had certainly made a clean sweep of our property, as they had driven off nearly all our horses, amounting to about a hundred, an all our bullocks and milking cows, amounting to over two hundred head of cattle.

About three leagues from Monte Molino they had fallen in with some unfortunate natives, who after bringing down wood from the Monte to burn our bricks, were returning to Saladillo; the savages instantly pounced upon them, carrying off both the bullocks and their drivers.

The loss of our stock was, of course, a great blow to me; but the only thing to be done was to go out to the estancia, in spite of the advice of my native friends in Frayle Muerto; 'No se vaya, Don Ricardo, los Indios están todavía en el campo; es muy peligroso'.* As soon, however, as our carts arrived, we again loaded our goods, and early in the morning started off for the camp, making an easy stage to the Arbol Chato† estancia, where we slept, as we had a long way to go next day to our own estancia. We kept pretty near the carts, in case any of the Indians should still be about. On this occasion, however, they went straight off; and none of the other settlers suffered, or indeed saw anything of them, except the Monte de la Leña party, as they passed near enough to be seen by them, though on the other side of the river. T. and his party rode down to the banks, and fired a few long shots at the nearest, but they were too far off for the bullets to take any effect.

As soon as we got near the estancia, I galloped on in advance of the train of carts, and found the place so much changed, from all that had been clone during my absence, that I should hardly have known it again. I of course found Frank and all the rest of the party in very low spirits at our misfortunes; and the particulars of the raid were again recounted to me. The loss of our horses, especially, was most keenly felt by us all, as there were some very good ones among them, and very few had been saved. Those sent into Frayle Muerto to us were luckily pretty good ones. Our working bullocks were also all gone, excepting those with the carts; and

*'Dont go, Don Ricardo, the Indians are still in the camp; it is very dangerous'.

† 'Flat tree'; there being a tree with a peculiar flat top near.

our loss altogether was a very heavy one, as besides the actual loss of money, the want of horses and bullocks made us lose what was even more valuable - our time, it being impossible at once to replace them. As soon as we had condoled with each other on our troubles, I proceeded to inspect the new house, which was very nearly completed. It consisted of two rooms on the ground floor, with a small passage between them, in which was the staircase. Above these were two more rooms, and a third story of one room was built over one half of the house. The second story was completed, but not yet roofed in, and the whole was finished about a month after my return. The house was about fifty-four feet long, by eighteen in breadth, so we had plenty of room. Our object in building a third story - a very uncommon practice in the country - was to obtain a good look-out place for surveying the surrounding camp. We were very much pleased with our new house, which was an object of great admiration to all the surrounding settlers. We did not, however, get into it until about two months later.

The two Englishmen, Henry and Tom, greeted me warmly, and I was glad to find both of them much pleased with life in the camp. Henry had already begun to operate on a square enclosure of a hundred and fifty yards, which with some assistance from the others he had made look more like a garden than anything we had before possessed. His promising crop had been very much damaged by a terrific hailstorm, a few days before our arrival, which had devastated the country. The hailstones were about the size of pigeon-eggs, and cut all the vegetables to pieces. This was rather disheartening, and did not much raise the spirits of estancieros who had almost at the same moment seen all their live stock disappear. The hailstorms in the Pampas are at times very bad, and the stones occasionally so large that they have been even known to kill lambs. The thunderstorms in summer are very frequent, as well as extremely violent. Soon after my brother's arrival in the country he happened to be at the fonda in Frayle Muerto during an unusually severe one, when the lightning struck the next room, which happily was empty at the moment. The effect produced on those in the adjoining apartment was as if a shell had suddenly burst close by; but fortunately no one was hurt, the only damage done being that another hole in the roof was added to the already existing fissures.

Violent gales of wind are very common in the Pampas, and there is, of course, nothing to break the force of them over these flat plains. But, as I daresay all my readers know, there is much more wind altogether in the southern hemisphere than in the northern, in consequence of the water so much predominating there over the land, and when the traveller gets as far south as the Auckland Isles all almost incessant gale blows round the world. On the other hand, one-third less of rain falls in the southern than in the northern hemisphere. Throughout the country the north wind in the summer is very disagreeable, as it brings down such intense heat, and a cool gale from the southward is always greeted with delight, though it is the certain precursor of a thunderstorm; which nearly always begins with a violent wind accompanied by dust, followed by heavy thunder, lightning and rain.

These dust storms, or pamperos, as they are called, are very bad in parts of Buenos Ayres, and sometimes last for several hours, during which time it becomes so dark that it is almost impossible to see anything; besides which, the cutting way in which the dust drives into one's face, feeling almost like a shower of little stones, quite blinds one. One of the hardest pamperos I ever remember to have experienced was nearly fatal to the roof of our iron house. The discomfited inmates suddenly perceived that the wind was rapidly lifting off the top of their abode, and it was only by instantly rushing out, and getting several lassos thrown over the roof, which were firmly secured to the ground, that we managed to save it.

I found a new addition to the live stock (which it was fortunately out of the power of the Indians to carry off) in the shape of a flourishing colony of ten or twelve pigs, which we now considered to be a sure road to wealth, some very wise and enterprising person halving calculated that the produce of two pigs ought in ten years time to produce at least a million. These profitable animals were half English bred, and had been purchased by my brother in Rosario some months before. Hume had undertaken to bring them up from Rosario, and to see them put into our carts. A good deal of difficulty was experienced in getting them safely from the train to the fonda, and having escaped from their new proprietors, they were seen careering wildly through the streets of Frayle Muerto with Hume and a train of small boys in pursuit, the latter highly delighted at seeing the gringo (foreigner) unable to manage his charge. They were, however, at length captured and brought to the fonda, where they were put into one of our carts, and despatched to Monte Molino, amusing themselves on the way by eating the bottom out of it. Pig-breeding is a thing that might with care be made to pay very well, as ham and bacon always command a good price. Up to the present time we have always found our small herd of pigs very profitable, maize being so cheap, and easily grown, and affording excellent food for fattening them.

The rams seemed very comfortable at first in their new quarters, and used to make themselves quite at home, walking in and out of the house in the tamest manner possible, making investigations into all corners of the place for Indian corn, of which they were exceedingly fond.

During my absence, our German puestero, Harry, who had now been with us more than a year, had moved from our house to a puesto which had been built for him, close to the river, about a mile from the new house. A puesto simply means an outlying station, and the puestero is, of course, the man in charge of the flock.

Harry had one of our flocks containing over a thousand sheep, on shares, and had been living down at our house in a rancho, until his own abode was built. This had been completed while I was away, and consisted of one room of about five yards square, with an azotea roof, and a very large ditch all round it, about twelve feet wide and twelve deep. Harry was one of those wanderers often to be met with in the colonies; he was by birth a German, but had begun life as a sailor in the English merchant service, after which he had served in the American navy. The various changes of life had at length brought him to Buenos Ayres, and there he resolved to turn shepherd, and had been several years in the country, having some time previously been companion with our first workman, Jack, in a puesto on the site where Monte de la Lèña now stands, managing a flock there for a proprietor, Jose Ribanca, a resident in Frayle Muerto, in fact the postmaster who supplied travellers with such excellent horses. Besides the sheep, they had a crop of wheat, and some pigs, but after a very narrow escape from the Indians they were forced to abandon their little settlement, and it was, perhaps, there that such a wholesome dread of Indians was implanted in Jack's mind.

Harry, looked well after the sheep, and, like most sailors, was a handy fellow about many things. He was very respectable, trustworthy, and, what was still rarer, sober; and we thought ourselves fortunate in having got him to act as puestero, as it was no easy matter to find anyone who liked living down in our wild neighbourhood.

We packed all our visitors, somehow or other, into the iron house, and prepared for the shearing. Walter had returned about a fortnight after my arrival, so we were eleven in number besides the servants, and required but few extra hands, as we made up altogether a party of about twenty.

CHAPTER XV

SHEARING - OUR NEW HOUSE - THE INDIANS AGAIN.

As we had not yet had time to construct the regular galpon or shed, under which the shearing generally takes place, we had run up as good a temporary shed for the purpose as possible, and, with the help of the shade of our few trees just outside the ditch, we made a very fair place there for our operations. The corral, where one of our flocks was generally shut in at night, being close to these trees, we had only to make another little pen, into which a small number of sheep could be driven ready to be caught for the shearers. There was an opening from this small pen to the boarded floor upon which the shearing took place. A certain number of men were told off for catching and tying the sheep, which were then laid on the floor, ready to be shorn. The shearers, as they finish each sheep, let the victim go, and call out, 'Lata', or 'Vellon', as the case may be. Lata meaning the tally which served out for every vellon or fleece, and so called because it is generally made of a small piece of tin (lata) stamped with the mark of the estancia. The serving out of the latas is the business of one of the masters, who, of course, before giving a tally sees that the fleece is lifted up by the man whose work it is to collect them, and deposited on the table, where it is rolled up and tied. It does not answer to employ a novice for this work, as he is liable to be deceived by the shearers, who are up to all sorts of trickery, by having a fleece presented to him in two portions. Experienced men will sometimes shear as many as a hundred and fifty or more sheep in a day; and I have been told, though I cannot vouch for the truth of it, that a man and his wife once sheared two hundred and ninety in a day, the women being quite as good shearers as the men, and doing the work much more neatly, seldom cutting the sheep, though they are not quite so rapid. A man is always at hand with a pot of tar and a brush, and when a sheep is badly cut, the shearer calls out for the medico to supply some of this soothing ointment. When a sheep is very badly cut the master stops the lata, as it is the only way of controlling the Gauchos who would otherwise gash the poor animals, quite regardless of anything but the number of latas they might make in a day.

We had on this occasion about four thousand sheep, so our shearing was only on a small scale; but this short description will give some idea of the South American wool harvest; it lasted about five days, during which time we worked from dawn to dusk, only stopping for a very short siesta. The fleeces are tied on a table, and then put into a large woolsack suspended by the mouth to a beam overhead (when, as in the present instance, the estancia does not possess a wool-press). The sack is swung clear of the ground and a few fleeces put in, after which a man gets into the sack and treads the wool down, more wool is added, and the operation continued until the sack is filled; the head of the treader rising gradually out of the sack as it becomes full, much like the figure in the old child's toy of 'Jack in the box'. One of our visitors undertook this operation, which he performed with the greatest perseverance.

As soon as the shearing was finished we took one load or wool into Frayle Muerto, where we had already sold it. Wool had fallen since last shearing, but we got as good a price in Frayle Muerto as was given in any part of the Republic. This fall in the wool market was, of course, a serious evil for all sheep-farmers. The close of the American war, which had now for some little time enabled the usual supply of cotton to be again transmitted to Europe, was the chief cause of this depression; and the great temporary rise in the price of wool, in consequence of the war, having caused numbers of settlers throughout the world to begin sheep-farming during the last few years, made the supply much larger than the present demand. This, like any other matter of demand and supply, will, of course, right itself in time; but reflections of this nature, though very satisfactory to a political economist or a chancellor of the exchequer, are no great consolation to a struggling settler, whose whole yearly income depends on the price of wool. It was, however, no more use to deplore this than any of our other misfortunes; and, having for some months clearly seen what was coming upon the sheep-farmer, we had resolved to turn our principal attention to agriculture, which promised to pay very well, merely keeping on our present flocks. The price of wheat in the River Plate was at this time quite as high as in England. The Paraguayan war had in part contributed to this; but it requires no artificial stimulus to make corn-growing one of the most paying speculations in the country.

We could not, however, depend for this purpose on native labour alone, and had, therefore, written home for more workmen from England to assist in our farming operations; and four men, from our old neighbourhood in Warwickshire, having at once volunteered to come out, we heard about this time that they were already on their way, and, likely to arrive at Monte Molino early in January.

About a week before Christmas the house was ready to receive us, and we prepared to bid adieu to our old abode and remove everything to the new estancia. A couple of days were sufficient for removing all our goods, including the iron house itself, which, after everything was cleared out of it, was taken to pieces and conveyed to the new estancia, where the sheets of iron served for roofing to some of the out-buildings. These had not as yet been begun; but, according to the plan we had made, were all to be built round a square of ground at the back of the house. In the centre of this yard was the new well, over which a pump had been placed, this being one of the trifling commissions I had executed in Buenos Ayres. The out-buildings included rooms for our men, a store-room, granary, stables, harness-room, galpon, carpenter's shed, hen-house, &c.; and the entrance of the yard was secured by a strong iron gate, which we brought up from the old house. The kitchen also, which was at the end of the house, was not yet finished, and in the meantime we used one of our sitting-rooms for culinary purposes. All these buildings, of course, took some time to construct, but, when finished, they made the estancia very complete.

It was indeed a joyful moment when the labours of moving were concluded and we were finally settled in the new house; for, although it was not quite completed according to European ideas - the walls not being plastered, no floors down, and a ladder still our only staircase - yet, to people who had lived for two years, without floors or plastering, in a dwelling which freely admitted not only the winds of heaven, but also its waters, the present strong weather-tight abode was a palace of comfort.

We now began preparing for Christmas; and, the larder being in a very empty state, the whole household went off on foraging parties in different directions, some going out with their guns in search of wild fowl, and some to Frayle Muerto for flour and other stores; and, the few cattle who had escaped the Indians having been by this time all eaten, my brother, accompanied by Lisada (who had again returned to us), went out campearing, as it is called; that is, looking for any stray animals who might have wandered back after the Indian raid. After about twenty miles riding, under a burning sun, they fell in with some wandering bullocks, and, after an exhausting day, drove them up to Monte Molino, where the prospect of some beef for our Christmas dinner was hailed with much delight. We had invited several neighbours to spend the day, and made up altogether a party of fourteen; passing it in a more cheerful manner than the first Christmas-day which Frank and I had spent in this part of the world. Tom provided us with a dinner which would have done credit to any chef, and we all drank success to Monte Molino. Our newly-finished mansion was much admired by our guests. Four of our visitors departed the following morning, and I went back with them to Monte de la Lèña for a day or two, after which I returned to Monte Molino.

Wishing to begin the new year well, I got up about sunrise on January 1, 1868; and, being the first awake, was occupying myself alone just outside the house, when I saw Lorenzo (the only one of our peons who was left on the place, all the others having gone into Frayle Muerto for a few days' holiday) galloping over from the old house, where he had been sleeping in the rancho, to look after the flock which was still in the corral there. As soon as the boy came near I saw that he was in a great state of excitement, as he was waving about a drawn sword and shouting out, 'Los Indios! Los Indios!' He told me they were at the puesto; and I, accordingly, ran up to the look-out place, hastily waking the rest of the party as I rushed through the house. I soon made out in the distance a very large body of men and horses, but whether or not all were mounted we could not clearly see. As far as we could judge, however, their number seemed to amount to about a thousand; but they were too far for us to distinguish for a certainty how many of the horses had riders.

Lorenzo then told us that, having got up very early, he espied the Indians in the distance, and had instantly run out to drive our working bullocks into the corral, firmly fastening the gate. A few of the Indians had then ridden up within two or three hundred yards of the wire fencing round the new house, and had driven away our few remaining horses. He watched them ride on towards the puesto (where Harry, is I before said, was living by himself), and then at once got on his horse and galloped up to give the alarm.

We now felt very anxious about Harry's fate; and, after watching the Indians in the distance for about half an hour, we had just determined to ride over to the puesto on our only two horses, when we saw a figure on foot slowly approaching from the same direction. This soon proved to be

Harry, in a very peculiar costume, consisting only of his calzones and a sheep-skin. We were much relieved to see him, and he soon proceeded, after being clothed and refreshed, to recount his adventures. He told us that, about two hours before daylight, he was suddenly awakened by a violent barking from his dogs, and, hastily slipping on his clothes, went up to the roof of his house. From thence he could just make out, in the dim light, a number of mounted men, one of whom called out to him in Spanish to come down, as they wanted to speak to him. He enquired who they were, and the same voice replied that they were Indians, of some tribe whose name he could not quite catch, but it sounded like Ranqueles. These were our usual visitors; but we afterwards discovered that this horde belonged to a different tribe, and that they were also joined by a large party of Gauchos from the south of Buenos Ayres. Poor Harry was very unwilling to descend among his unwelcome visitors, and thought at first of making a fight of it, as his house was well defended by the deep ditch, and he had arms and ammunition. The man who was conversing with him, and who proved to be the interpreter, told him, however, that he would do better to come down to them, as, in that case he should not be hurt; but that, if he resisted, they would burn his house and murder him; and that, as they were a strong party and had fire-arms, he had no chance of holding out against them. It was still too dark for him to see their real numbers, and, being quite alone, he at last resolved to trust to their promises and go down.

He accordingly went out, and the cacique began questioning him through the interpreter as to the number of soldiers in Frayle Muerto, how many we were at Monte Molino, and whether the party consisted of foreigners or natives; also whether anyone was living at the old house, and other questions, which proved that their spies had previously been about, and had obtained a great deal of information. Harry told them the truth about all these things, only suppressing the fact of there being anyone at the old house, and it was probably owing to this that Lorenzo escaped.

The cacique then told him that they wanted to find the passage across the river, and ordered him to mount, behind him, which he at once did. They then rode down to the river, which was much swollen by the late rains, Harry pointing out the place where the ford was. On the way there they passed through a large body of men amounting, as it appeared to him, to at least five hundred.

When they reached the river, the cacique told him to get on an old horse and proceed through the ford, which he did, closely followed by three or four Indians, who had previously relieved him of his boots and shirt, no doubt thinking it a pity that they should get wet. The river in some places is extremely muddy, and unless one hits off the exact spot where the pass is, one is apt to get bogged. This, between the darkness and the rather novel position in which he found himself, Harry on the present occasion failed to do, and he and his four companions soon stuck fast in the mud. His sensations were not very agreeable, as he was afraid the Indians might think he was trying to deceive them, and he fully expected to feel one of their long lances stuck into him. He, however, explained as well as he could that it was accidental; and they all floundered back, somehow or other, to the place whence they had started. Their second attempt was more successful, as they got safely across, though the river was so full that they were forced to swim their horses over. The cacique then called to them to return, as the river was too deep for the whole party to attempt to cross it. He informed Harry that he might depart, as his services were not wanted any longer; but advised him to conceal himself in the long reeds, lest he should fall in with any stray Indians, who, according to their usual merciful habits, would probably kill him.

Harry did not require a second bidding, and as soon as they had all ridden off in the direction of the puesto, the troop having been called together by the sound of a bugle, he lost no time in crossing the river, thinking that he would be safer on the opposite side, and then hid himself among the reeds. Here he waited until it was quite light, when he thought he might venture back to his puesto, to see what damage had been done. He waded back through the river, and seeing no more of the Indians, walked to his house, where he found that everything he possessed in the world had been carried of, and that all the sheep had disappeared. His horses were gone, of course, so he had nothing better to do than to walk up to the house and relate his adventures.

The Indians, who were at a great distance when we first saw them, had quite disappeared by this time; and having only two horses on the place, it was useless to attempt any pursuit. This driving off of sheep was quite a new feature in Indian attacks, and proved how large a body there must have been for them to venture on such a step. About twelve hundred of our sheep were gone, and there were no apparent means of getting them back.

Later in the day, Harry, having recovered his morning adventures, and being again clothed like a respectable puestero, sallied out on one of the two remaining horses to see whether he could find any traces of his stolen flock. The rest of our party remained disconsolately at home, only wishing that the Indians would reappear, and give us a chance of acknowledging their attentions. Harry returned towards evening, and told us he had traced the sheep a long way to the south, of course taking care not to come up with the Indians. The course they had taken was marked by the dead bodies of many of his beloved flock, having small pieces hacked out of them, which had apparently been eaten quite raw, as there were no signs of any fire having been lighted. This led us to suppose that the Indians had merely driven off the sheep to kill by the way, and not with the intention of getting them down to their own country.

About five hundred of our flock returned to us the next day, appearing none the worse for their little expedition to the south, though they must have traversed a good many leagues in the course of their travels; and their arrival was warmly greeted by their bereaved masters, but no more was ever seen of the remaining seven hundred.

Harry stayed at the house after this, with the small remnant of his flock, naturally enough not caring to return to the puesto.

Early every morning we took a good survey of the country, hoping some of our horses might find their way back to us; and on the 4th of January a small number of animals being suddenly descried at a considerable distance, Harry and Lorenzo rode of to see what they were. We were just outside the house, busy at work finishing some of the new fencing when our servant Tom, who from the roof of the house was watching the proceedings of Harry and Lorenzo with the deepest interest, suddenly called to us that he saw them both returning at full gallop, pursued by a number of Indians. We rushed in for our rifles, and ran out to meet the Indians, fearing they might overtake the two men, but very soon saw that the latter were too much in advance for there to be any danger of this happening. We stopped, therefore, and remained not far from the house, waiting till the Indians should come close enough for us to get a good shot at them. Harry and Lorenzo soon rode up, the Indians following at about a quarter of a mile behind, until they saw that their prey had escaped them, when they changed their direction, some of them riding up towards the spot where our few remaining bullocks were feeding, evidently with the intention of driving them off. The bullocks were luckily in the enclosure we had just made, with wire fencing round it, which was, of course, invisible from a distance; but when the Indians came near enough to see it, they all stopped short, appearing very much astonished at this new kind of hedge.

Being a small party, and evidently afraid to come up to the estancia, they then turned and rode back towards the site of the old house. We should now most likely have had a good shot at them, as they were about to pass within range, but one of our party, getting excited, fired too soon and the Indians instantly altered their course. We all fired after this, but as far as we could perceive, our shots took no effect, though we could see them strike the ground pretty close to the Indians. The rest of the Indians were in the meantime beginning to drive off our sheep, who were almost half a mile from the house. This we should soon have put a stop to, by sallying out on foot, but when the first shot was fired they desisted from their endeavour, and all joined their companions, the whole party riding down to the old house, where they remained a short time, endeavouring to find something to carry off, after having just stationed one of their number on the top of the rancho to act as a sentinel.

There being nothing for the Indians to carry off, it did not seem worth while to go out against them, as we had only two tired horses, while they were all as usual very well mounted, and we could not expect to catch them on foot. Had we only had our horses we might easily have finished them off, as they were but a small party, and we were all well armed. They soon rode away, having on this occasion done us no harm, and we saw no more of them for some time; none of our neighbours suffered from this invasion, which seemed to have been directed against us, the Indians having no doubt, previously made as complete an inspection of our premises as they dared.

A few days after this Lisada returned from Frayle Muerto, and luckily brought a few horses back with him, so that we were relieved from our sort of forced residence at home. Harry left us soon after to go to Rosario, where he hoped to find employment, his Indian experiences having finally disgusted him with camp life, which, indeed, was not surprising; but one of our visitors volunteered to remain and become our puestero, a very usual way for new-comers to learn some experience of settling, the puestero taking the flocks on share, and receiving a third of the profits.

We had been endeavouring long before this to stir up the neighbourhood to unite in an expedition against the Indians, and we now made a great effort to get an armed force together, intending to go down to the Indian territory, and try to give them a lesson which might stop these repeated invasions, as it was impossible we could put up much longer with the present state of things. But our efforts were all unsuccessful, and the many difficulties in the way proved too great; the chief one being that the settlers, though most ready to fight with the Indians, did not like leaving their property quite undefended during their absence, lest, while they were in pursuit of one body of Indians, another should take the opportunity of carrying off everything they possessed. We were again forced, therefore, to have recourse to petitioning the Government for some protection of the frontier, though with very little hope of success; as we had already sent in numerous applications of a similar nature, to which General Mitré was too much occupied with the Paraguayans to pay any attention. But as the proposed expedition seemed impracticable, we again got up a strong memorial, which we despatched to the English Minister at Buenos Ayres, though without much hope of its producing any effect.

After this experience of life in the Frayle Muerto camps, my readers will not be surprised to hear that none of our visitors cared to remain except the intrepid puestero: all the others departed in search of a more peaceful spot to settle in, and business obliging me to go down to Rosario, one of them who intended to visit Entre Rios accompanied me there, assisting me by the way in taking the rest of the wool down to Frayle Muerto, where we disposed of it for as good a price as could now be reasonably expected.

CHAPTER XVI

THE CHOLERA - LAST SIGHT OF THE INDIANS - ELECTION OF THE PRESIDENT.

The first news that greeted our arrival in Frayle Muerto was that the cholera was again raging in Rosario, and, indeed, everywhere throughout the country. At Villa Nueva a great number of the foreigners employed on the railway had died of it. It appeared to have assumed the form of the worst kind of Asiatic cholera, and was something beyond all belief. In Cordoba more than eight hundred a day were dying, out of a population of a few thousands, and in a monastic college there thirty-two out of the forty inmates had died. It was at this moment very bad in Frayle Muerto, and there was little else for anyone to speak of but the terrible state of things throughout the country. At a few leagues distance from Frayle Muerto the railway conductor pointed out to us a dead body lying not far from the tramway, which he told us was that of a tropero (a man travelling with mules), who having been attacked by the disease, was stripped and left to die by his heartless companions. We heard many melancholy instances of this sort of desertion, cowardly relations and friends leaving the person attacked to perish without any effort for his recovery or relief, beyond a jug of water placed at his side; and the guard related one curious case of this description, in particular. A few days before, he had seen, when passing near Villa Nueva, a ma lying by the side of the railway, apparently dead, with a large demajuana of water placed near him; on the second day, however, the man had disappeared, and the guard found on enquiry that he had recovered from his deathlike state almost miraculously, and without any care or attention from his friends, beyond the jug of cold water which they had put near him when first he fell down there.

On reaching Rosario I found the town in a very disorderly state, as, notwithstanding the cholera, the Federal party had taken this opportunity of getting up a revolution, and the place was in their hands.

Two English gunboats had been summoned by our consul, from Buenos Ayres, to protect the British interests, as one of the Argentine gunboats having been fired into by the rebels, they had begun bombarding the town, and the shots had entered several houses, and greatly alarmed the peaceable inhabitants. I had only been a few hours in Rosario when I heard that one of the Las Rosas partners, who had been for a short time in England, had just returned, and while walking from the station to the town I met the whole party, just landed from the river steamer, and on their way to the station, accompanied by the commander of the Doterel (one of the gunboats), and escorted by a guard of marines.

The formed rather an imposing procession, as besides my friends at Las Rosas, the English officer and his men, the party included six or seven new acquaintance just arrived in the country, a thoroughbred horse fresh from England, a short-horned bull named Whirlwind, and about twenty sheep, two or three carts laden with luggage closing the cavalcade. They all stopped on seeing me, and told me they were going out next day to Las Rosas, where they pressed me to accompany them, and though I could not do this, I promised to follow as soon as I should have finished the business which brought me to Rosario. In the meantime I accepted a kind invitation from the commander of the Doterel to stay on board his ship, and was not sorry to pass the night outside a town where both cholera and a revolution were going on at the same time.

I was glad to find our old puestero, Harry, had got a comfortable place at an English stable, and I saw him there in the evening looking very well and happy; but next morning I heard from the owner of the stable that poor Harry, who had been sent out to the quinta to cut some alfalfa for the horses, had been suddenly taken very ill there with the cholera, and his master begged me to come out with him to the place where he was, which was about two miles from the town. We accordingly rode there as fast as possible, taking with us all the remedies we could think of, and found poor Harry in a small house belonging to the quinta, lying on the bed there. We tried every possible means we could to restore him, applying mustard poultices, rubbing his hands and feet, and giving him port wine, brandy, and chlorodyne; but almost the first glance had convinced us that the case was hopeless, as his hands were already tinged with the deathlike blue colour which in this terrible disease is one of the fatal symptoms. Harry was quite conscious, and much pleased to see me, but very desponding about himself, though we did all we could to cheer him up and encourage him, but it was evident he thought himself dying. He was, very anxious to see a doctor, and at his earnest request I at length went back to the town to try whether I could not persuade one to come out. This I found impossible, as they were already almost worked to death, and one of the cleverest doctors in Rosario had that day died himself of cholera.

They were also unwilling to run the risk of being stopped by the soldiers outside the town, who, indeed, had detained me some time before I could convince them that I was in no ways concerned in the revolution. From the symptoms I described also they assured me that by this time all was probably over, but they gave me several prescriptions, which I took to the chemist and had made up, sending them out to the quinta, where the messenger found that poor Harry had died a quarter of an hour after I quitted him. He had then shaken hands with me, and taken an affectionate farewell, and I only left him in consequence of his earnest request. He had been a faithful friend, and I believe felt a real attachment to us, and his sad death grieved us all much.

The cholera now became hourly worse in Rosario; the town, in the streets unoccupied by the soldiers was like a city of the dead,- whole rows of houses where the inhabitants had died being shut up. Every one who could do so escaped to the camp, where an unfortunate French family were carried off by the Indians. The cholera this year attacked foreigners quite as much as natives, and throughout the country people were dying at the rate of one out of every ten. After a couple of days on board the Doterel, I went out to Las Rosas, and found all the party still at their station, the Cañada de Gomez, waiting for their carts, which arrived there a few minutes after I did. We then set to work to load them, and despatched them to Las Rosas late in the day, intending to follow ourselves the next morning.

According to the usual custom we laid down in the waiting-room, and were roused from our slumbers, rather early in the morning, by the sound of a train rumbling through at a most unusual time, and found that it had been despatched to Mendoza, to bring down troops to subdue the Revolutionary party. We had, luckily, shunted the trucks, used for bringing down all the Las Rosas' goods, to a siding, the passengers assisting in these sort of matters in this free and enlightened Republic; but our having done so was a perfect chance, as no train was expected till the following morning.

We rode out next morning to Las Rosas, and found everything safely arrived; and, our spirits rising at this welcome change from the sad scenes we had left in Rosario, we passed a pleasant day, telling our various adventures.

The next morning, however, I felt myself very unwell, and soon found I had a severe attack of cholera, which lasted, rather badly, for about twenty-four hours, during which time my kind friends applied every possible remedy; I then took a good turn, and was soon well.

I stayed on a few days at Las Rosas, all sorts of rumours reaching us meantime about the progress of the Revolutionary party; one report being that the rebels had been endeavouring to destroy the railway-bridge over the Carcarañal, so as to prevent the arrival of soldiers from Mendoza; and this proved so far true, that the rails had actually been pulled up and the traffic stopped for some days; it was repaired after a short time, and the troops then reached Rosario, of which they immediately took possession, the Federal army retreating outside the town, where they formed an encampment.

As soon as the railway was repaired, I returned to Rosario, the train proceeding cautiously towards the bridge, as we were uncertain whether or not the rails had been again disturbed; so we all stood, ready to jump out in case of necessity; but our passage was quite uninterrupted, and we safely reached the town, where we found everyone in full expectation of a pitched battle outside the walls, to add to the horrors inside; this expectation was disappointed, as, in a day or two, the rebels quietly laid down their arms, having apparently thought better of it. Meanwhile the cholera became worse and worse, not only in the town, but even in the camp outside, where it was committing fearful ravages; at Cañada de Gomez it was terribly bad, whole families dying of it, and, out of a small German Colony there of twenty-five, eighteen died. To give a little idea of the state of despondency which people reached, I may mention an unhappy estanciero, who, after having seen everyone else die in his house in succession, was himself attacked by the disease, and shot himself in despair. No one can imagine the depression throughout the country, and nothing in Europe in late days can give an idea of the state of things. The English escaped this year no more than anyone else; and we heard dreadful accounts of the state of things among the prosperous estancieros to the south of Buenos Ayres, where I had spent such a pleasant time last year; though, I am thankful to say, my kind hosts there escaped; but whole estancias were deserted, and we were told of flocks wandering about without any owners, the country being half depopulated. The Buenos Ayres papers contained nothing but one long list of deaths; and the whole Republic was in a state of mourning, those who had escaped themselves having to lament some dear friend or other. The usual mixture of self-devotion, springing from one class of minds, was exhibited, in strong contrast to the most heartless conduct from the other; and the fear of infection became so great, that the dead were buried with the most indecent haste, the nearest relatives often not daring to enter the house, where the unhappy victim had been left to perish alone, but lassoing the dead body from outside, and dragging it out, as rapidly as possible, to the hastily-made grave. There was no temptation to remain in Rosario, and, the moment my business was concluded, I returned to Frayle Muerto, where I found the cholera very bad, and the people dying in numbers, the priest, as I before mentioned exerting himself nobly to assuage the sufferings of his poor parishioners. On returning to Monte Molino, I heard that half the population of Saladillo had died during my absence; but this was the nearest point to us which the cholera reached, and all the estancias round us escaped entirely. My readers can imagine the delight of leaving the close atmosphere of the plague-stricken town for the fresh pure air of the open camp. I found on reaching home that my brother, uneasy at the accounts which reached him, had gone down to Rosario in search of me, somehow missing me by the way; and it was with great pleasure we saw him safely return, a few days later, though he brought still worse accounts, if possible, of the state of things, and news, which grieved us most deeply, of the sudden death of one of our greatest friends from cholera. The disease, however, began to abate towards the middle of February, and disappeared with the cold weather, never again, I hope, to return to a country where previously it was quite unknown.

I found things going on pretty well at Monte Molino, where our four new workmen had arrived during my absence. They seemed very favourably impressed with the general aspect of camp life, the shooting and riding quite reconciling them to the solitary neighbourhood, and they had got safely up the country, in spite of revolutions and cholera.

A short time after our return from Rosario my brother and I had the last sight of the Indians with which we have been favoured so far, though on this point one never likes to boast. Our larder was again in a low state, and, being tired of living on armadillo, and not liking to kill our sheep if we could avoid it, we went out on a campearing expedition to the south. We were about sixteen miles from home, 'mas o ménos', and had captured two rather lean cows, which we were slowly but triumphantly driving home, when, happening suddenly to look round (a thing which, indeed, one did pretty often), a very unpleasant sight met our eyes. We beheld in the distance a large body of mares, watched by several men on horseback, whom we, of course, knew must be Indians; and, while we were looking at the party through our field-glasses, a still larger body of horsemen hove in sight, driving before them a number of animals, evidently with the intention of joining the troop we had first seen. We now thought there was no more time to be lost, and turned at once towards home, hoping the Indians might not see us. Our horses were rather tired, but we got them along somehow or other, urging on the cows, whom we resolved not to abandon if we could help it.

After riding a few miles, with rather uncomfortable sensations, we were relieved to find that we gradually lost sight of the Indians, and, rather late in the day, we safely reached home with our two prisoners.

The excitement in Rosario, which had led to the revolution, was chiefly owing to the approaching election of a new president, which was to take place early in May, and to which we were all looking forward with much anxiety; and, in spite of the temporary re-establishment of order, a severe struggle between the Federal party and the Government was expected, as great agitation was going on throughout the Republic. Contrary, however, to all expectation, the election passed off quietly, and Don Domingo Sarmiento was elected president or the Argentine Republic. This choice gave general satisfaction throughout the country, and was hailed with especial joy by all the English settlers, as Señor Sarmiento is distinguished not only for his great abilities, but even more so for his wise and enlightened views, and the earnest zeal for the good of his country, which his disinterested conduct in public life lids always shown. He had been lately residing in the United States, where he had filled the important office of minister; and his election as president was entirely unsolicited on his own part, he having refused all entreaties from his friends, to return home, in order to become a candidate for popular favour.

The able manner in which he ha carried on the Government has hitherto quite fulfilled these sanguine hopes; and, as far as regards the interests of the English settlers, I may add that the latest accounts from Frayle Muerto report - though, its I fear, prematurely - that troops are already being despatched to protect the frontier from Indians invasions.

CHAPTER XVII

WE BEGIN PLOUGHING - ENGLISH TRAVELLERS - A MYSTERIOUS ROBBERY - LISADA'S ADVENTURES - FERTILITY OF THE SOIL - RETURN TO ENGLAND

Having now determined to give our chief attention to agriculture, we set to work to prepare our land for the wheat-sowing, which would take place about the end of June, and purchased about twenty additional bullocks for ploughing with. We found breaking these in extremely hard work, as they were all young animals; and no one unacquainted with bullocks can possibly imagine the degree to which they can try one's patience. The Scripture comparison, of a 'bullock unaccustomed to the yoke', must recur very forcibly to anyone unlucky enough to have the training of these animals. The natives say of them, what old naval officers used to say of the seamen, that they will not obey a command unless it is accompanied by a few strong adjectives; and, certainly if the use of them is at all effective, the Gauchos ought to find their bullocks most obedient servants. Our new team used to make a rush in every direction but the right one, refusing to go straight along the furrow, and, after entangling themselves together, would kick like horses, further manifesting their disgust at their new occupation by violently plunging about; all which manoeuvres were rather disturbing to the course of the plough.

We reduced them to order at last; but they are always obstinate and tiresome to manage, and seem to be possessed by the republican and restless spirit of the country, which Hume used to declare infected the very animals. We had purchased some American ploughs, until we could import some from England, and found them answer very well. The native plough is, I should think, much the same sort of instrument as that which one imagines Romulus to have used for the celebrated ploughing round the site of his new city. It consists only of a large log of wood, with a piece of pointed iron at one end, which, of course, does not plough the ground at all, according to our ideas, but merely scratches it up; this, however, the natives consider quite sufficient for all purposes of cultivation, and, in this rich and beautiful soil, decent crops really are produced in this extraordinary manner.

M. returned from England in April, bringing out his steam plough, everything on his estate having been got ready during his absence for commencing operations there on an extensive plan. The first trial of the plough was, however, to take place close to the station at Frayle Muerto; and there was great excitement about it in the neighbourhood, a large number of persons collecting to see how this first experiment would answer. It succeeded very fairly indeed, considering the very bad nature of the spot of ground chosen, which was full of biscacha holes, and roots from the monte close by. M. at once began ploughing at his estancia on a very large scale; and though it was too late for wheat sowing that season, by the time his ground was prepared, he got in a very large quantity of maize, which promised to produce a very good crop.

We worked hard at our less scientific style of agriculture, and had generally four or five ploughs going, each drawn by two or four bullocks, according to the state of the ground. Before beginning to plough it was necessary to burn the grass, for which, of course, the estanciero always waits until the wind is in a favourable direction. Burning the camp at other times, to improve the grass, is a very common practice, and camp fires from this, or accidental causes, are constantly to be seen all over the country, and at night have a very picturesque effect. The grass is always, if possible, burnt down just before rain; after which a beautiful crop of the finest green, to which both sheep and cattle are extremely partial, springs up directly. These fires last sometimes for two or three days; but in our part of the country there was not the least danger from them, as they could easily be beaten out with sheepskins if they appeared likely to approach any spot where they could do harm, and there being nothing substantial to feed the flames, they are so trifling, that I have constantly galloped through the few yards over which they extend when I have happened to meet them. But in parts of the province of Buenos Ayres, where whole tracts of land are covered by enormous forests of thistles ten or twelve feet in height, these fires become very dangerous when the thistles are ripe, and occasionally cause very serious consequences. We were quite free from thistles in our part of the country, and very thankful to be so.

Our ploughing progressed so rapidly, that about the beginning of June I went up with a neighbour to Villa Nueva, to purchase some seed wheat there, which we had been told was ver good. On my return from Villa Nueva I stayed for a day or two in Frayle Muerto, and found there a young English gentleman attached to the Embassy at Buenos Ayres, who was travelling through the country, accompanied by his sister, she being certainly the first young English lady who has had the courage to come out to the Argentine Republic for a tour of pleasure. They were on their way to Cordoba; and as it would have been unpleasant for a lady to stay at the post-houses on the way, the fonda at Frayle Muerto, which I have described, being very far above the average, they had brought with them their own tents, in which they lived, travelling through the country in a sort of open curricle. Two of our friends were with them, and the whole party were attended by a very hideous little negro, who was generally supposed to have been purchased at St. Vincent for half-a-crown.

Pompey was about twelve years old, and when perched up on an enormous recado, on a very high horse, where he looked perfectly happy, bore a very strong resemblance to at monkey. The travellers intended to make a long expedition up the country, but finally went no farther than Cordoba. They talked of paying us a visit on their way up, but the fear of Indians in the camp prevented their accomplishing this; and delighted as we should have been to have had a visit from them, we could not conscientiously press Mr. and Miss ---------- very strongly to come out to Monte Molino.

After parting with the travellers, I despatched my wheat early in the day to Monte Molino in the carts which had been sent out to fetch it, and followed it the same evening, sleeping at an estancia not far front the Arbol Chato intending to catch up the carts next day, and reach home with them; but the first thing that greeted me in the morning, was a messenger from Las Chañaritas informing me that my carts had the night before been pillaged by the Indians, and that the peons had made their escape to S.'s estancia there. I accordingly rode to Las Chañaritas (S. was just then away in England), and found the two peons there, who at once proceeded to give an account of the affair. They told me that, on the preceding evening, they had just reached the usual spot chosen as a halfway resting-place between Frayle Muerto and our estancia, and which consisted of a small group of quebracho trees (the only trees to be found along the whole sixteen leagues of road), and were just about to tie up the bullocks for the night, when four

Indians, armed with long lances, rode up, and began to rob the carts, taking also some of the peons' clothes from them. They then proceeded to light a fire under the carts, with the benevolent intention of burning whatever they could not take away; but the fire luckily soon went out, and the only thing actually burnt wits a box, containing a small tabby kitten, which had just been given to me by a lady in Frayle Muerto. Whether the poor kitten was really burnt I do not know, but from the appearance of the charred remains of the box, I felt some hopes it might first have been broken open, and the luckless little prisoner have made its escape into the long grass. On hearing this unpleasant news, I borrowed a horse from S.'s estancia and despatched one of the peons on it to Monte Molino, to fetch some more bullocks to draw the wheat, the Indians having, of course, driven off those attached to the carts. I then rode over with a friend to inspect the scene of the robbery, which was only a league from Las Chañaritas. I found everything scattered about in all directions; but the wheat had luckily escaped, and as soon as the bullocks arrived, we got it safely home; nor was our eventual loss very great, as shortly after our arrival at Monte Molino the eight missing bullocks trotted gaily up to their usual paddock, munch to the delight of their masters. Their return greatly confirmed the doubts already felt as to the robbers being really Indians; and the peons soon after leaving us, to go to Frayle Muerto, saying they were afraid to drive the carts any more, we had them closely watched for some time, though without any result; but we always believed them to have been in league with the robbers, whom we did not, for several reasons, suppose to be Indians.

Ploughing is an occupation which has a good deal of sameness in it, the chief variety being that of occasionally turning up a snake, which I need hardly say was instantly despatched; and I have sometimes killed as many as twelve in a morning, a pair of strong boots quite securing one from any danger from their attacks. The wheat-sowing was a welcome change of work and we began it about the end of June. We had no drill, and were, of course, obliged to sow broadcast. During this time immense flocks of pigeons, doves, and parrots were always hovering about us, though we had scarcely ever seen any before, except in the montes. How they discovered what was going on I never could imagine, as the nearest monte was quite thirty miles off, and no wood-pigeons had ever been seen on our property before, though a solitary parrot would sometimes find its way down there. They came in such dense flocks, that I have sometimes killed eight or ten at one shot. They were very useful for pies, &c., and during the sowing-time we almost lived on them, in return for which they ate a good deal of our wheat. When the seed was all in the ground they vanished directly, but were always on the spot when any maize or wheat-sowing, was going on, though by what means they knew of our proceedings it was quite impossible to guess.

Meanwhile Henry was diligently working at our garden, which promised to supply us well with vegetables. All those which are ordinarily seen in English gardens grow here in the greatest luxuriance, some of them attaining an immense size. The radishes especially might have suited the inhabitants of Brobdingnag, as among those left for seed I pulled up one measuring more than eighteen inches in circumference. It is scarcely necessary to add that we did not eat radishes which had attained these dimensions. Melons, pumpkins, and cucumbers are raised without difficulty; onions also flourish in the most wonderful way, and if our animals had only multiplied as quickly as our vegetables, we should have grown rapidly rich. We planted about a thousand peach trees round our house, intending them to form in time a small monte, the peach growing more rapidly here than any other tree, and beginning after three years' growth to bear fruit. My readers can easily imagine the beauty of a grove of peaches covered with the lovely pink blossom; and the gardens round Rosario used to look in spring much like the descriptions one reads of the groves of Ispahan. We planted, also, quantities of poplars, willows, ombre, paraiso trees, and a great many others, besides long hedges, round our newly-ploughed land, of sino sino, a kind of acacia, which grows very rapidly; it has thorns of the most formidable description, very thick foliage, and bunches of pretty yellow flowers, a good deal like laburnum, and in a few years forms a capital hedge, quite impervious to any animal with which I am acquainted. We also made hedges of cactus, the common sort which one sees generally in Italy, and which always reminds me of the backs of hair-brushes. It springs up round any hut, or erection, and grew round our old house, as soon as we put it up; but it is a little more difficult to manage than sino sino. The other sorts of cactus, with long, rope-like leaves and beautiful scarlet blossoms, are found wild in the montes; but there are very few wild flowers in the open camp, the scarlet and purple verbenas, which grow in enormous patches, looking like pieces of red or violet carpet rolled out on the grass, being the commonest. In the montes the flowers are lovely, and the climate is extremely well suited for all kinds of plants.

We now began to plant some flowers in our garden, which soon looked very gay; and indeed a very few years' growth of flowers and trees will make the estancias round Frayle Muerto as attractive as any place in the world.

Our poor rams did not, however, find the pampas, in spite of all these delights, at all suitable to their health; they seemed very happy at first, but after some weeks one of them became ill; his throat swelled, and in spite of the most affectionate attentions from his proprietors, he soon died. We fancied he had been bitten by a snake, or, perhaps, by one of the enormous spiders I have mentioned; but I think this was not the case, as all his companions gradually followed him, to our sincere sorrow, and I think their death put the final touch to our disgust at sheep-farming, which is certainly not a very profitable occupation just now. Of course if the breed of sheep could be really improved, it would become just as lucrative here as in England; but a great deal of care is required for the acclimatisation of European sheep, and we certainly were not very lucky in our experiments.

We had for a long time been endeavouring to get an English clergyman appointed as chaplain to the district round Frayle Muerto the nearest English service being at Buenos Ayres, and therefore of no use to us; but it was not till April 1868 that a clergyman was sent by the South American Missionary Society to Rosario and the surrounding camps. We held a short service in our house every Sunday morning for our own people, but were all very glad when we heard that henceforth the Rosario chaplain was to perform the service once in every month at one of the estancias near Frayle Muerto. The first place he officiated at was the Algarobitas; and the service there was very well attended, about forty people being collected, some of whom had ridden nearly thirty miles to be present at the first English service held in this wild part of the pampas. It was arranged that the chaplain should take all the estancias in turn, but we hope before long to have a resident clergyman in Frayle Muerto.

Soon after this there was again an alarm of Indians in the camp, though on this occasion they did not reach Monte Molino. Lisada, who had come down to us for a short visit, went out one day campearing, taking with him a small brother whom he had brought with him, generally known as Tanne, an abbreviation, I believe, of Stanislaus. They were looking out for stray cattle, when the Indians suddenly appeared, and pouncing upon Lisada, whose horse was too tired for him to attempt to escape, carried him of with them to act as vaqueano. Tanne, who was at some little distance when the

Indians rode up, being well mounted, made his escape, and got safely to S.'s estancia, where he related what had occurred, and poor Lisada was mourned for as dead by all his friends. I was in Frayle Muerto at the time, and about two days after this melancholy news reached me, was walking in the street, when I met a friend of Lisada's, who suddenly informed me that Lisada had just reappeared none the worse for his sojourn among the Indians. I went off to his house to see whether this was true, and found him safely returned, and very comfortable in bed, resting from his fatigues, as he had only come back very late the evening before. Lisada soon proceeded to relate his adventures, and told me that he had been seized by a party of about thirty Indians, who were soon joined by a much larger number. They informed him that he was required to act as a guide, and asked him where he came from. On learning that it was from Monte Molino they were very desirous he should take them down there, but he told them that in consequence of the frequent visits which we had lately had from their fellow-countrymen, there was really nothing worth their taking, as we had only a few horses and bullocks left; upon which they held a council, and soon resolved to go to the Esquina Ballasteros, a small village, near which was an estancia belonging to the father of Don Nasario, the Comandante at Frayle Muerto, and not far from which was M.'s property. When they got near the estancia they left Lisada with some of the Indians, the rest going up to attack the house. Shots were soon heard, and after a little time thick smoke began to rise from the house, showing too plainly that the unhappy party within had had the worst of it. The interpreter afterwards told Lisada that the place had been very bravely defended by two or three men and the negro servant, who acted as capataz, but the Indians at length got in and killed them all. After this they drove off every single head of horses, cattle, and even the sheep, intending the latter, no doubt, for provisions on the way. Soon after the destruction of the estancia, they caught an unfortunate Gaucho, who made a desperate effort to escape, and was only captured after several leagues' chase. This appeared to enrage the Indians very much, and after tying his hands together, they ordered him to kneel down, and in this position soon despatched him with their long lances.

Lisada's feelings while this was going on must have been anything but pleasant, but he dared not show the sympathy he felt for the poor man (who as a last request asked him for a cigarette) lest the Indians in their excited state should instantly turn upon him. Several of them, however, came up to him after this, telling him not to be afraid, as he was an 'hombre muy guapo' (a very brave man), and adding that they remembered him at Monte Molino, when we received them so kindly, and in return for this he should not be injured. They then gave him an old horse to ride away on, shook hands with him, and wished him good-bye, upon which he very willingly took leave of them, and made the best of his way back to Frayle Muerto, greatly overjoyed at this unexpected escape, upon which I warmly congratulated him.

I met M. Directly afterwards, who told me that the Indians had also been seen near his house, trying to drive off his horses, but upon the party within the house sallying out they instantly took to flight, and no more was seen of them. I then went to condole with Don Nasario on his family misfortunes, and tried hard to persuade him to get up an expedition against the Indians, who were supposed to be still in the neighbourhood, lying in wait for a tropilla of carts which were daily expected from Mendoza, robbing one of these caravans being one of the forms of pillage to which they were most partial, as it offered a very large booty combined with little danger of any resistance with firearms, the Gauchos being nearly as much afraid to use them as the Indians. Don Nasario, however, declined the expedition, saying that he could not get up a sufficient number of men, horses, or arms, and though several of the English settlers offered to accompany him, he was not to be induced to sally forth. His father, Don Benito, had, luckily for himself been in Frayle Muerto at the time of the attack on the estancia, and so escaped. It was of course more Don Nasarios's affair than ours, and seeing he was not to be persuaded, we let the matter rest.

Lisada, after this, remained in Frayle Muerto, where I believe him at this moment to be flourishing, unless he has been deported to the frontier, in compliance with a law prevailing in this part of the world, that any Argentine idling in the towns may be at once taken down to the frontier, where he is obliged to exert himself, the ruling powers in this country having, I suppose, the same objection to loafers which some of the English settlers fell. This law appears to me almost worthy of Plato' Ideal Republic but the Argentines have not yet quite reached the state of feeling in everything which he contemplated.

No more was seen of the Indians after this, and things went on very quietly for the next four months. Our wheat crop promised well, we ploughed up a large tract of land to be sown in November with maize, we seemed likely to have a large supply of potatoes, and our garden was in a very satisfactory state; our men worked well, and altogether the estancia again assumed a prosperous appearance. We had settled down in our new house into civilised ways, dining at sunset very comfortably together, and spending the evenings chiefly in reading the welcome supplies of books which our friends at home sent out to us from time to time. Hume was still detained en England, but James W. had returned to Monte de la Lèña, where he was warmly welcomed back by all his friends.

Our affairs being in this promising state I resolved to take this opportunity of paying a visit to England, and about the middle of October bade adieu to Monte Molino. My brother accompanied me, intending to see me off from Buenos Ayres. After wishing all my friends in the neighbourhood 'Good-bye', I went down to Frayle Muerto, and took leave of all the worthy inhabitants, promising to execute all sorts of commissions in England, one of which was to bring out for Lisada the most gorgeous poncho which money could purchase. He took an affectionate leave of me, wishing me 'buen viaje, y vuelve pronto' (a good journey and a speedy return). We stayed a few days at Las Rosas, and while waiting for our train at the Cañada de Gomez station, met S. just returning from Europe, accompanied by twelve young Englishmen, who had come out to settle close to him. He had agreed that they should rent small portions of his estate for agriculture, and they all intended to live close together, so as to form a strong body in case of any Indian attacks. This is certainly an excellent idea, and more likely to lead to a rapid settlement of the country than any other plan which has yet been devised. We wished all success to S. and his band of colonists, and went on to Buenos Ayres, where I quickly secured my passage on board the mail. My brother and two or three friends accompanied me on board, and as the Arno steamed slowly away I watched them sailing back to the mole with many wishes that they also were with me.

My voyage home was rapid and prosperous; in addition to the places touched at on our way out, we stopped at Pernambuco and St. Vincent. There is a curious natural breakwater of rocks at Pernambuco extending some miles along the shore, behind which is a small harbour. On the 2nd of December I again beheld the well-known headlands of the Isle of Wight, and we ran into Southampton that same afternoon. I at once landed myself and my luggage, which included a great variety of things of which I had taken charge, among them being a parrot who had lost his feathers in the course of the voyage, and numerous enquiries as to whether he felt the cold were made as I walked up the street at Southampton, carrying the unlucky foreigner on my wrist. The express train soon whirled me up to Waterloo, and I was once again amid all the well-known sights and sounds of the metropolis. The regular tramp of the policeman on his beat replaced the 'serenos' shouting the hour and state of the weather. Passengers pushed by, and omnibuses prepared to run over me, in a way very different from the stately tread of the Spaniards, and the slow procession of bullock carts. My revolver had become as useless as the arquebuses in the Tower, and, amid all the rush and roar of London, Indians, Gauchos, pampas, and estancias seemed fading away like a dream.

POSTSCRIPT

Having told the tale of my four years' experience in the Pampas, my readers may naturally ask, What is the moral of my story? Am I content with the country which I have adopted? And do I desire to recommend it to others? Or is it my object to proclaim that my enterprise is a failure, and should be a warning to my fellow-countrymen, either to stay at home, or else to choose some other part of the world in which to seek their fortunes? To these questions I readily reply; and, first of ally I must confess that if I and my companion had had four years ago the experience which we now have of the fine camp on the banks of the Saladillo, we should not have been so ready to pitch our tents there. Our distance from the little town of Frayle Muerto has added greatly to our labours; so has our position to the south of the Saladillo, making it necessary to cross that river, frequently with great difficulty, whenever we had occasion to go to Frayle Muerto, the Terceiro also being without a bridge till within thc last twelve months. The want of wood has also been a most serious embarrassment to us; and it has been laborious and costly to us to obtain it for our fencing and building. But our worst trouble of all has been the incursions of the Indians, and the serious losses which their depredations have entailed upon us, besides the consequent inability to increase our cattle. Admitting the serious nature of these three hindrances to our success, I must acknowledge that our selection of land was not a wise one.

On the other hand, it must be remembered that our chief object was to put on cattle largely, and sheep; and that, with no mistake about the excellence of our pastures, and also abundance of water in a river boundary of six miles, the only real impediment to our success has been the incursions of the Indians; for there is no difficulty in driving cattle to market, and our wool is easily conveyed to the rail. We cannot deny that we were told to expect such enemies; and we must admit, first, that we held them cheaper than was their due; and, secondly, that we trusted also to the good will and the power of the Government to protect us from them. But the long and unhappily protracted war with Paraguay has for some time past drained the Argentine Republic of all their soldiers; and the Government has been powerless to protect us. Our neighbours nearer Frayle Muerto have found a substitute for cattle and sheep-farming in the growth of wheat and maize, to which they are now adding flax. We took last year to the same resource, and ploughed forty acres for wheat, and ninety for maize. The first crop of wheat from land in the Pampas newly broken is seldom very good; but I learn that our yield of wheat has been sufficient to encourage us to grow more, and our maize crop was large. With the help of our wool we shall thus, I believe, this year pay our expenses. We hope next year to get in two hundred acres of wheat, besides a larger quantity of maize; and we shall probably make trial of flax also. I think it likely that a good thing may be done by this cultivation of the soil, apart from sheep and cattle; but it is to the combination of both that we now look for success. The Paraguayan war being virtually ended, we reckon confidently on the Government to protect us from the Indians. In times past presidents of the Republic have succeeded in altogether stopping for many continuous years those raids on both the natives and settlers; and things have now come to such a pass that the Government must come to our help, or else the confidence with which foreigners are flocking to those Pampas, to the increasing prosperity of the Republic, will be shaken, and the immigration stopped. Whenever such protection is awarded to us, we shall again give free scope to the increase of our cattle and our sheep. We may then hope to be no longer the only settlers to the south of the Saladillo, and with new neighbours new facilities both of traffic and communication are sure to spring up. Why should not those little jars marked Liebig, with which all good house-keepers in England are fast becoming familiar, be filled on the banks of the Saladillo, as well as on those of the Uruguay? And those cases of beef and mutton from Australia - why should we not supply them from the Pampas? Thus, notwithstanding our losses and discouragements, I see no reason to despair of our success; and, provided the Government will defend their frontiers from the Indians, I can still encourage others to come and settle in our neighbourhood. Where will they find pastures of so fine a quality to be purchased at so low a price; with a fine climate, and many of their fellow countrymen within easy reach; with a line of railroad, too, about thirty miles off, and a post by four mails monthly to England, of five weeks only from our little town to London? All that is wanted is our protection from the Indians. We have shown our trust in the Government by staking our fortunes in their country. We believe that with the return of peace they will think it their plain duty to grant us this protection.

We have great confidence in the newly-elected President, Señor Sarmiento, and we cannot believe that, with the power to help us, he will do us the injustice to leave us longer in our helpless condition.

INDEX

STOCKCERO

stockcero.com
Viamonte 1592 C1055ABD
Buenos Aires Argentina
54 11 4372 9322

stockcero@stockcero.com

www.ingramcontent.com/pod-product-compliance
Lightning Source LLC
Chambersburg PA
CBHW030811310726
48980CB00006B/461/J

* 9 7 8 9 8 7 2 0 5 0 6 6 5 *